Advance Praise for *1*

MW00528922

"The sly, deadpan humor in many of these stories is both charming and artful. Humor strikes me as one of the most elusive qualities in fiction, but to Robert Foreman comedy seems second nature. This is an impressive, highly original and satisfying collection."
–Christine Sneed, author of *The Virginity of Famous Men*

"Robert Long Foreman is an exciting and original new voice in fiction, which is abundantly evident in his thrilling debut collection, *I Am Here to Make Friends*. In the tradition of DeLillo and Saunders—and Foreman belongs in the company of such great writers—Foreman's characters are ordinary unsung people whose lives are made briefly interesting by a small unexpected change or phenomenon that slowly, hilariously, and poignantly spirals into absurdity. With a deft hand, Foreman spins sentences that are subtly surprising and vibrant with meaning. He's an acute observer of human nature, of the ironies and duplicities inherent in contemporary American culture. His wry wit is a gift that he deploys--like a literary weapon--to make you chuckle at his characters (ourselves), even as he stealthily breaks your heart with their thwarted longing. Foreman's *I am Here to Make Friends* is a brilliant and compelling collection by an exceptionally talented writer who reveals the weirdness in our day to day lives at this moment in history. This is a dazzling book."
–Maureen Stanton, author of *Body Leaping Backward: Memoir of a Delinquent Girlhood*

"Robert Long Foreman's stories are so smooth. They glide along as if on ice. No tricks, to twirls, no fancy moves. And then you realize that that ice is dangerously thin. Every story of Foreman's is two stories. There's the top story, the narrative itself. But underneath is another story, keeping pace, racing along, hyperventilating…The driest humor, the wildest imagination. Bizarre stuff told by the most matter-of-fact, deadpan narrators. In every story, Robert Long Foreman achieves what even the best bestselling authors fail to do: render the extraordinary ordinary; the ordinary, extraordinary."
–Sara Pritchard, author of *Crackpots (a novel)*

"Robert Long Foreman has a particular knack for instigating a curiosity in readers about things that they might not otherwise think to explore—guns, pigs, bug bites, childbirth, death dreams, and the strangest parts of human intuition. In his new collection, *I Am Here to Make Friends*, Foreman captivates us with each story, keeping us guessing about what will happen next and how we will respond to the actions of characters who remind us of ourselves and our friends—and the choices we would make only in secret. In crisp, compelling prose, this fiction collection's journey into the psyche is a multifaceted odyssey into the storytelling impulses and cravings that whisper within us in the quiet hours—and its uncanny allure keeps us turning page after page, anxious to know what revelry and revelations wait beyond each turn."
–Saba Syed Razvi, author of *In the Crocodile Gardens*

I Am Here to Make Friends

Sundress Publications • Knoxville, TN

Editor: Saba Razvi
Editorial Assistants: Anna Black, Erin Elizabeth Smith
Editorial Interns: Erica Hoffmeister, Steven
Sampson, Jacquelyn Scott

Colophon: This book is set in Calisto MT.

Cover Design: Kristen Ton

Book Design: Erin Elizabeth Smith

I Am Here to Make Friends
Robert Long Foreman

Acknowledgements

"Appraisals" was published by *Hobart* in 2014.

"Awe" won the 2016 Robert and Adele Schiff Prose Prize at *The Cincinnati Review* and appeared in issue 13.1 (2016).

"Cadiz, Missouri" appeared in *AGNI* issue 75 (2012) and *The Pushcart Prize XXXVIII: Best of the Small Presses 2014 Edition.*

"Lost Origins" was published in *The Chattahoochee Review* 36:2/3 (2016/17).

"The Man with the Nightmare Gun" won the 2013 *Willow Springs* Fiction Contest and appeared in issue 72 (2013).

"On Brian's Dreams of Submarines" appeared in *Mid-American Review* 33.2 (2013).

"Turkey of the Woods" appeared in *Indiana Review* 34.2 (2012).

"The Vinyl Canal" was featured in *Willow Springs* 81 (2018).

Table of Contents

for Stefanie

Awe

Gary said he would never be the same after watching his son get born.

"When Roger came out of Frances," he said, "I was in awe. I'm still in awe." He took a drink from his Longhammer IPA. "I'd been impressed with Frances. I'd been in love with her. I'd never been in awe. This is all-new."

"Wow," I said.

"That's right. I'm in awe of all women, now. I am! They look different. They smell different. You know how I always respected them. Now it goes beyond that. Way beyond."

Gary was right. Respect was one thing. But awe? When was the last time I'd felt that?

I knew when. It was when my friend Kel showed me his collection of books that had titles that went like, The Somebody's Someone. That was how he described it. And that was what it was: a tall bookshelf full of books titled *The Pirate's Daughter, Ahab's Wife, The Memory Keeper's Daughter, The Orphan Master's Son, The Time-Traveler's Wife, The Mathematician's Wife, The Pilot's Wife, The Heartmourner's Wife, Omensetter's Luck, The Chronicler's Son, The Twice-Dragon's Son, The President's Wife*. There were a hundred books there, Kel assured me, as I stood looking at them with my mouth open.

I told Gary about Kel's shelf, the last thing that made me feel awe. He said I must be easily awed. But no, I said. It had been two years since Kel showed me his shelf. So no way, Garé.

"Seeing Roger get born, though," he said. "It changed my life. I recommend it."

"You do?"

"Yeah."

"Wait, what?"

"What?"

"What do you recommend?"

"Seeing a woman give birth. In person. It's not the same, on video. You've got to go out and find the real thing, whatever you have to do. It's like a painting. It's not the same when you see it in a book or a movie. It's astounding."

Astounding. These were strong words.

Maybe he was right, I thought, and I could use some awe in my life. It was making Gary glow. What could it do for me?

I tried Craigslist, in the M4MW personals section. The ad I wrote said:

Healthy man—educated, enough to use commas and dashes—looking to watch woman deliver baby. Not a sex-thing—just don't know where else to look. Drug/disease free. Promise not to vape in delivery room. Man must be HUNG, no less than 8.5".

That last part was a joke I worried people might not get. I wasn't worried enough to cut it from the ad.

I got responses but not what I was looking for. Not at all. I couldn't figure out what half of the responders wanted—sex, I guess. They wrote in Craigslist code.

So I thought I'd try looking in a bigger town—a city, even—with an ad I'd edited to its bare essentials. No jokes. In a city, I thought, there must be two people willing to let me be a part of the most significant moment of their lives so far. Or just one person; a single mom would be great.

Within three days of posting the ad on the Craigslist of the nearest city—San Francisco—I had thirty responses. At least four were legitimate. Two had photos of the couples attached. One had an ultrasound image of the unborn baby.

I didn't write back to everyone. Why bother? There was no need to look further than Ben and Janet for my power couple, my awe-inducers. They looked great in their photo: smiling, fully clothed, out on a hike in what looked like Yellowstone, Ben a little older than Janet, not enough to make it weird. In his photo, their fetus was looking in the direction of the ultrasound wand, his eye like a hollowed-out marble, his half-formed face inquisitive.

We met on neutral ground: a Starbucks near their house, how near I didn't know. I didn't ask. I had to drive two hours to get there, so I hoped this was the jackpot.

"We're not 100% sure Ben's the father," said Janet at our table by the window.

"Really?" I said.

"No," she laughed. "Not really. He's the dad. But we have," she said with a half-smile, "an unconventional marriage."

"Like an open marriage?"

"Exactly like that."

They seemed to think, like all the open-marriagers I've met, that she and Ben were the only ones who had an open marriage, like they invented it. They're not, though, and they didn't. Ben-Hur had an open marriage.

"That's what it is," Ben agreed, with what I thought was less enthusiasm than Janet. Maybe I was projecting.

"Okay," said Janet, with the palms of her hands together, not in prayer. "We have some questions. About your needs. My needs have been on our minds so much these days, it's actually nice to have a break from that. You know?" I didn't. "We know where the birth will take place. It's a home birth." As she said this, Janet watched to see how I reacted. But I smiled and nodded, because I think home births are incredible.

"It might pose a problem, though," Ben said.

"Yeah," agreed Janet. "We're not sure totally sure we have enough outlets."

"That sucks."

"We brought photos," she said, whipping out her phone, "since we're not *quite* ready to invite you over." She showed me a series of photos, then, of a room I gathered was their bedroom; it had a bed in it, and decorations that go with open marriages. There was a poster for something, maybe a sexy movie, with French writing on it. Something hanging over their bed looked like an electronic dream catcher. As Janet swiped through the photos, I soon found I was looking at photos of walls with power outlets in them. I spent half a minute looking at close-ups of outlets.

Not knowing how to react, I looked at Ben and nodded.

"So," he said. "You won't need a generator. For the equipment? And what will you need to bring exactly? Just cameras and lights?"

"Oh," I said. "I'm not filming anything. This isn't a filming thing."

I'd never seen two expectant parents look so puzzled at the same time. "I don't understand," said Janet. "You wanted to film this for a documentary."

There are two kinds of people, I thought then: those who will say, "I thought you wanted ____," and those who'll say, "You wanted ____."

"You are," Janet said, "a documentary filmmaker. Aren't you?"

I put my hand to my forehead.

Not quite a year prior to then, I had sworn off documentary filmmaking. I had changed everything in my life: moved into a new apartment, gone vegan, stopped talking to my mother. I did not think to remove "Documentary Filmmaker" from my email signature. Janet must have seen it, once we started corresponding, and gotten the wrong idea. I couldn't blame her for that.

"I haven't touched a camera in a year," I said. "Not since my last subject. She died. She killed herself." With a half-smile, I said, "I guess that's what I get for making a film about people on the brink of suicide."

"So you want to see me give birth out of—what—curiosity?"

"Yeah," I said, nodding, brightening. "I heard about it from Gary—my friend. About what a mindfuck it is." I was paraphrasing. "I mean, how much it changes you to be in the room when someone's getting born. Gary's a different guy, now—in a good way."

"And you need that."

"Sure."

"Because of the suicide?"

"Because of my subject, yes. That's part of it." I looked at the table.

I thought this was the end. I would have to write back to the naked couple who sent me a photo of themselves against a plain white wall with no clothes on, one of them very pregnant. They said they were having a nude birth and I would have to be okay with that. Starting now, I guess.

Ben and Janet excused themselves to go talk things over. I said, "No, it's fine. It's a lot to ask. You can text me later if you don't want to decide now." But they said they only needed a minute.

They moved to the next table to discuss it, but at Starbucks the tables are close together, and Ben and Janet spoke at a regular conversational volume, so I could hear everything they said. I turned my back to them and sat watching the sun stream through the front window—my god, they keep the windows clean at Starbucks, I thought—while I listened to them talk about me.

"I don't know," Ben said.

"I don't know, either," said Janet.

"He seems nice."

"He needs our help."

"I don't dis*like* him. But we don't *know* him."

"We don't *know* him, but we could *help* him."

"We *could*."

"We could and we should," said Janet. "We're sharing our cord blood with strangers. It's not like we would be selective about that. What's so different about this?"

A lot, I thought, but they went on talking a while longer as I watched cars pull in and out of the parking lot and the sun kept streaming through the window. It was just the right time of day to sit in that Starbucks.

Maybe because of their open marriage they were open to things generally, were the kind of people who would do well on a commune. It may have helped that everyone involved was white. But they agreed to let me watch the birth.

"We're glad to have you aboard," said Janet, smiling, and kind of lowering one eyebrow slyly. I wondered if it was a smile she would have given me had we met under other circumstances—were she not pregnant, and were I not, in her eyes, a broken man in need of proximity to birth. There was no way she was attracted to me; she was about to have Ben's baby. But under other circumstances, would she have been? I didn't know.

"I'm honored," I said, trying to look in all their eyes at once, for maximum earnestness. But it isn't possible to do that. "Thank you so much," I said.

I thought it would make sense to spend more time with Ben and Janet prior to the labor; I barely knew them. But I didn't want to push that. I didn't want to invade their lives any more than I had arranged to. So I didn't see them for a while. I would talk on the phone with Janet, when she called to ask if I was still interested, and to ask other questions, like how long would it take me to get there, and could I bring clean towels in case they needed extras. We would talk for half an hour at a time, about our lives and things in general. We had probably—I don't know—a dozen such conversations in the two weeks that followed our first meeting.

I think Janet was at loose ends. Ben was working long hours—he's a corporate attorney for Charmin. And it's not like he's always been as attentive to her needs as she's needed him to be, like last fall when her sister was in a near-fatal traffic accident and instead of rushing home from work to get Janet and drive them to Portland he said, on the phone, still at work, "Do you think you'll have to go see her, then?"

Nobody's perfect. That's what I told Janet. I reminded her that everyone will fail you a little bit. Sometimes it happens at the worst time, but it's inevitable.

When Janet told me where Ben worked, I thought she said he was a corporate attorney for Charmaine.

"Who's Charmaine?" I said.

"Not Charmaine," laughed Janet. "Charmin. You need to get your ears checked."

"I need to get my everything checked," I said.

We laughed about that a long time.

I would ask sometimes to make sure she and Ben were still okay with letting me watch her give birth.

"Of *course* we are," said Janet. "We're looking forward to it. Even if you don't want to put us in a movie."

17

"I'm honored," I said for the second time in ten days. "I'm honored you would let me be a part of this." You've got to be careful how many times you say you're honored. It could lose its effect.

Janet said, "There will be four people at the birth: my mother, you, Ben and the midwife."

Was it significant, I wondered, that she listed me before Ben?

No, I thought.

Five days later, Janet went into labor. At three in the morning, she texted me: "Luke's coming."

I got my batch of clean, white towels and put them in my car. I brought my overnight bag, which I'd packed in advance, in case Luke took his time getting born.

Settling behind the wheel of the car in the dark of that early morning, I thought of things that could go wrong. Luke could be stillborn. Janet could change her mind about wanting to be a mom. The midwife could turn out to be an abortionist or an arsonist. I would be there for it.

More reasons, I thought, not to film the thing. I counted to fifty and turned the key.

I got there without a problem. There was a tunnel I had to drive through to get there, and as I approached it, I considered driving headfirst into the wall—not because I wanted to die, but because death is never far away and I knew it.

Rather than invite grief into the lives of my loved ones, I went through the tunnel.

~

Janet had given me their address. They were finally ready to let me into their home, which, it turned out, was big and old.

18

I didn't think they had such old-looking houses in this part of the country. It looked eighteenth-century, so it must have been made to look old without really being old—but they must have built it long enough ago that it did look convincingly old. It looked colonial, but also Modern, as if Frank Lloyd Wright had designed it after banging his head and forgetting what century he lived in.

When I knocked, Ben answered their door, which was redder, taller, and thicker than the doors I was used to. "Now *that* is a *big door*," I said when Ben opened it. I don't think he got the reference.

Ben looked grim. I was afraid for a moment. "You're here," he said. "You made it."

"Everything all right?" I had my arms full of the towels and a present for Luke in a bag: a little, brown bear.

"We're fine," he said. "We don't need the towels. Janet's mom brought some."

I walked back to my Accord, then, and put the towels in the trunk. Ben watched. I heard him take deep, loud breaths. Birds chirped. I went back and entered the house, Ben holding the door open. He was a big guy, a little over six feet, with a closely trimmed beard and eyes like Rasputin that must have served him well at Charmin World Headquarters.

There were two impressions I had of the house interior. One was that the hardwood floors were top-notch—near-reflective. The other was that Janet was screaming and howling upstairs. "No!" she cried—then, "Oh! No!"

"Is she all right?" I asked.

"She's fine," Ben said. "I guess she sounds like that when delivering."

"The things you learn about a woman."

Ben frowned. He didn't seem to be incredibly happy about what was happening. I asked if he was all right.

19

"Yeah," he said. "Oh, yeah. Just a little stunned." He put his hand to his forehead. His hand shook.

An older woman entered the room. She looked like Janet, so much so that it was as if Janet had had the baby and suddenly it aged thirty years. The woman was her mother.

I shouldn't have mentioned it, but I said, "You look just like Janet. I mean, wow."

"You must be Bill," she said. Then she walked away. It was me and Ben again.

"Is she all right?"

He nodded. "She's shy," he said.

I knew she wasn't really shy. But I was there for Ben and Janet, not Janet's mom, and I knew I was welcome at Ben and Janet World Headquarters. No worries.

I almost laughed when I saw Janet, up in her and Ben's bedroom, she looked so much like a woman does in a movie when she goes into labor. Her face was red, her hair wet with sweat.

She was hard at work, expelling a whole infant from her body—an undertaking for anyone, but especially for someone as little as Janet. She was small and skinny, one of those women whose bodies hardly change when they get pregnant, except that their bellies get huge. It's astounding.

When Janet saw me, she said, "Bill! Thank god!" And she gestured me over and squeezed my hand. She looked into my eyes with desperation, or fear, or apprehension. All three, probably, plus other things I don't have names for, as I have never been in labor and haven't had to struggle to find words for them. She squeezed my hand hard and shut her eyes and screamed. People almost never do that when I touch their hands.

The midwife suggested Janet change positions. "Movement, Janet. Movement," she said. She had greying

20

hair and incredible skin. She exuded good health, like all midwives do, like she must condition her hair with ginger root extract and eat food that's more organic than life itself.

I wish I could look half as healthy as a midwife. What's their secret? Is it that their job is to witness the miracle of birth several times a day, every day? Do they get more sleep than the rest of us?

Ben said, "Let's go settle." On the way downstairs, he said Janet would be a while, that the midwife had said Luke's birth would take hours. He didn't say when it was she'd said that.

The place he took me to settle was the basement, where he had a little bar, with stools and everything. They had art down there I didn't care for, a TV, and a treadmill. Ben gestured to a stool. He stood behind the bar and poured us whiskeys.

"Whoa," I said.

"We gotta get ready."

"I don't know."

Ben said, "Relax," and there was something about the way he said it that made me relax indeed. If he'd been holding a gun, it would have been a sign of danger; he was holding a drink, though, so it was permission to let it ride.

I sat at his bar, put my hands on its edge, and looked up into his face. The floor was higher behind the bar than it was in the rest of the room, and as I have mentioned, Ben was tall. I felt like a kid, then, looking up at a grown man who was serving me whiskey.

"What's on your mind?" Ben asked.

"My mind?"

"Yeah."

"Not a lot. I drove over here."

"But what do you think of all this?"

"Your house?"

"Sure."

"It's nice! You have a bar. Come here often?"

"I do."

"I've always wondered that. About people who have house bars. I think if I had one, I would never use it. I'd drink in a chair."

"Yeah?"

"Or in bed, maybe?"

"You ever drink in bed?"

"No."

"Huh."

"I don't think it's *ever* happened, now that I think about it. But, so, what's going on with you? How's your head? I mean, how's life? There's a lot happening upstairs." We could hear Janet scream every five minutes. "It's like somebody's having a baby up there," I said.

"My head's fine," said Big Ben between big sips of big whiskey. "Life's fine. It's weird, though. Shit's about to change."

"No kidding."

"Everything's about to change!" He leaned back, against the wall. "I don't know. I like the way things are now."

"You wanted kids, right? You planned this?"

"Of course. But look back here." I leaned over to see what I thought I'd see behind Ben's bar: bottles. He said, "How long's it gonna be before I have to move these?"

"Oh, right, because—"

"Because Luke will be old enough to come back here."

"And reach the bottles."

"And mix himself a Tom Collins. Six weeks later he's a heroin addict."

"That's true. It's a slippery slope." I took a deep breath and said, "That was one big part of Anna's story, actually. The subject of my film, I mean. Who killed herself?"

22

"Yeah?"

"Bad choices. Bad friends. Real tragedy."

I was about to tell him how her father had tried to convince her to kill herself, long before she went through with it, when she was just a teenager, with a knife he bought her for her seventeenth birthday, so she could kill herself with it. But we were interrupted, we fellas at the bar, by Janet's mom. Standing in the doorway, looking at Ben, she said, "Janet is transitioning." I hoped I might learn from Ben's facial expression what that meant. What was Janet transitioning into? Would I soon meet Janet the Butterfly?

"I'll be right up," Ben said to Janet's mom's back. "Stay here," he said, turning to me. "Help yourself. I'll be back."

In the twenty minutes Ben was gone, I finished my drink and had another. I looked a long time at their painting of a big, red semicolon, or whatever it was. Janet's wailing sounded more insistent the emptier my glass became. Where before the screaming stopped for a while, then started again, now it kept up, like it wasn't coming from a woman but from a planet, like the wailing of a woman in labor was the cosmic sound of gravitational pull. I wasn't drunk.

As the wailing got shriller, I wondered if they had forgotten about me down there—which suggested new possibilities for my life. I could stay in the basement a long, long time. I could paint them another semicolon.

But I didn't want to do that; I don't even like semicolons; so I put down my drink and went to the bathroom—which smelled like peach—and walked upstairs to the bedroom where Janet was about to not be pregnant anymore.

I knew that in order to see Luke get born I would have to see Janet's vagina. I hadn't really thought about it, though; I hadn't wanted to. Janet wasn't a vagina to me, she was a human being, with a brain and a heart, and a life and a sister in Portland who would be there later, after I'd gone. But in addition to those things, Janet did have a vagina. There was no denying it, by the time I'd reached the top of the stairs. She was on her hands and knees, and her vagina was facing the door I walked through. It made me feel self-conscious about walking through the door; there I was, just another guy who would have to pass through an opening that day. Janet was wailing and wailing. The midwife was watching Janet's vagina; her mother was stroking her hair to reassure her top half; and Ben was standing by the midwife, looking lost.

I went up beside Ben and patted him on the arm. He said, "Bill! Hey."

"What's up, Ben," I said. "How you holding up?"

"I'm all *right*," he said. "It's gonna happen."

"It won't be long, now," agreed the midwife, not looking at either of us.

"It's weird," Ben said, his arms folded across his chest.

"What's weird?"

"I just feel like, you spend half your life trying to resolve all your bullshit. Then you spend the other half giving bullshit to someone else, for him to figure out."

Janet's mom scowled at Ben. I smiled at Janet's mom.

"But there are good things, too," I said as Janet wailed louder than ever. "It's not all bullshit." When she was done with her next outburst, I added, "There are good times. Good memories."

"That's *true*," Ben said, looking down.

We were silent for a moment, until I said, "She wasn't my wife. The woman who killed herself."

Ben looked at me.

"She wasn't pregnant."

"Okay."

"Ben," said Janet's mother, gesturing. "Take over?"

Ben left to take over stroking Janet's hair. Janet's mother went into the adjoining bathroom. She was sweating. It was hot in there, and being in the room with Janet made you feel like you exerted yourself. When Janet's mom came back, I kind of waved and said, "Hey." She just looked at me and then went back to Janet's head.

Ben came back. All the color was gone from his face, except white, and I guess brown, because of his brown beard and brown eyes and eyebrows. He looked like he was about to faint, which would have been bad. I wasn't big enough to catch Ben. I took him by the arm into the hallway.

"I think," he said, "I need another drink."

"You need a glass of water," I said. "Can I get you one?"

He nodded.

Their sink! It was deep. It was beautiful. My sink was half the size of theirs, and theirs had a filter on the faucet. Only the cleanest water for their new baby boy. I filled a glass with clear, cool water, and took it up to Ben. I almost took a drink myself, it looked so clear and good, like it came from a mountain spring.

When I handed the water to Ben, I said, "That's some *sink!*"

"Just put it in last month," he said between gulps. "Thanks."

I put up my hands and snorted, like it was no big deal, which it wasn't, and took the glass from him.

It was then I realized Ben was crying.

Here he was, about to be a father, weeping away and afraid of how his life was changing while he still lived it, and here I was, talking about his sink. Janet was making noises in the bedroom that I knew from TV were pushing. And the midwife was yelling, "Push!" Which was another clue. So I knew we had to get in there.

Ben was crying with his mouth open, leaning against the wall and paralyzed with fear.

I had to do something, and not just because I wanted to get in there and be filled with awe. This was Ben's big moment, too, and I wasn't about to let him miss it.

I considered slapping Ben on his face. I didn't, which was good.

I put my hand on Ben's shoulder.

I didn't tell him about the tape Anna made of her suicide, in which she swallowed pill after pill and a big glass of water, glancing at the camera with the deep, dark eyes she could barely keep open once she'd overdosed. She kept rubbing her face with her left hand until, sitting on her bed, with the camera pointed at her like a death ray, she leaned back, mumbling and humming a song I'd never heard, fading out on the TV in my living room while I sat on my couch with my hand on my mouth and watched her die.

She wanted me to have the tape, and I do. The police brought it to my door. She wanted me to use it in my documentary. I will not. Of course I will not.

I didn't tell Ben that death and birth are so near to one another I don't know how to live with them. I didn't say that filming Luke as he was born would make a perfect circle I did not want to complete. It would answer the film of Anna's death like a correction, implicating Luke in an act of mourning as soon as he was brought into this world. What cruelty.

I looked Ben in his tear-soaked eyes. "Ben," I said, squeezing his big arm. "Go in and meet your son."

~

If you look up the word "awe," like I did before I went in search of the thing it refers to, you see that it's about

26

reverence. When you're awed, you are put in your place by something greater than yourself.

Awe is about dread. It's about being nearly crushed by something you don't understand. Awe makes no guarantees; it could make you reborn, or it could squeeze the life from you. So of course Ben was afraid of the awful thing that was happening in the next room.

I don't mean "awful" as in bad. The word "awful" is like the word "awe." It used to be spelled "awefull." You're supposed to call something "awful" when it fills you with awe, not when you don't like it. An awful thing frightens you and fills you with wonder at the same time.

And so the birth of Luke was awful. It was everything Gary had said it would be. One moment there were four of us in the room, and then, with one last push, we were five. We were in tears.

I think it was the "we" that I wept for. I heard Luke cry before I saw his face, and I felt his cry in my heart. I recognized him. I recognized his need. I knew he was Luke the moment I heard his voice, knew his heart was beating with the rest of ours. He had joined the human race.

Ben cried. Janet's mom cried. Janet cried and held Luke, who crapped all over Janet. Ben held her hand and laughed at that, with tears in his eyes, and got a towel. The midwife took a drink from her bottled water and kind of smiled. This was every day of her life, watching this happen. What a job. What a life. Janet's mother faced the window with her hands together, maybe in prayer.

That was how I left them, thinking, Kel's bookshelf was shit compared to this. I don't know what I felt when I saw Kel's shelf. It wasn't awe.

I went down to their kitchen to dry my eyes and have a drink of their great, great water. I washed a few dishes because I can't leave dirty dishes in a sink under any circumstances. I left a note on the pad of paper on their fridge that said, "<u>Great</u> sink!", and I went to my car to drive home a changed man. I had come face-to-face with something awful, and like Luke, like Ben, like Gary, Frances, Roger, Kel and Janet, her mom and the midwife, and everyone in every car I passed on the highway on my way home, I was alive.

Appraisals

I went to the Antiques Roadshow with my mother's
green marble frog in the inside pocket of the jacket of the
black suit I wore to her funeral that morning. I had taken
the frog from her house. I wanted to know what it was
worth.

It was worth nothing, said the man in the green blazer
with no tie, but every shirt button fastened. He said it from
the other side of a small table where we sat poised as if
playing a strange game of chess in which the only piece in
play was the marble frog. He had a beard but no bedside
manner. I asked what he could tell me about the frog.
"Nothing," he said again, and beckoned to the man behind
me, who had claimed, sometime in the three hours we had
spent standing together in line, that the cobbler's toolset in
the canvas bag that hung from his arm was "just ancient!"

The convention center's bartender was also just ancient. I
thought he was making some kind of joke when he asked,
as he mixed my Old Fashioned, if the painting he had kept
in his garage for the last twenty years was worth anything.
He tried to describe the painting to me. It sounded like what
he had in his garage might not be a painting.

It was not a pleasant bar. It was too bright. You could
walk from the convention hall and into the bar and not
know you were in a bar. It was like an airport lounge, and
the cocktail was about as good as it would have been at an
airport.

I was drinking at a small table when a man who had clearly spent the last half-decade letting himself go approached in a polo shirt and said he would like a "second opinion"—on what, he didn't say. "Please," he said. From a paper bag he withdrew a metal Crayola box and placed it at the center of the table. He gave me a grave, reticent look that made me feel for a moment like I hadn't left the funeral. He asked what I could tell him about the box.

I took a drink and lifted the box, expecting it to be heavier than it was. "I thought it would be heavier," I said. "It must be tin?" He kept watching, kept silent. I opened the box. There was nothing inside. I closed the lid and rotated the box in my hands. I found a stamp on its base, with a date: 1920. I said, "It's from 1920," and the man nodded as if I had not just read it off the box.

I began to understand what was happening. I sat back. I said, "How much did the other appraiser say this was worth?"

"Five bucks," the man said, curtly, and looked at me with his mouth closed.

I said, "I estimate its value somewhere between twenty and twenty-five dollars."

The man didn't look happy, exactly, but he looked less dejected than he had when he sat down. He thanked me, took his box and paper bag, and nodded to the man who replaced him.

This next man was also wearing a polo shirt. He was a talker. He told a long story about a ceramic vase that he sat on the table between us. It was a blue and white vase, a few feet wide and rather tall, so that when he spoke, I couldn't see him. All I could see was the vase. He said the appraiser "in the other room" was a "nice enough guy," but what he'd said about the vase didn't square with what he'd read in the "guidebooks." I didn't ask him what guidebooks on vases were like, though it was all I thought about for the ten minutes he spent telling me how he came to own the vase. His story ended when he said, "But the guy out there told me, 'Sir, I'm afraid this was made recently. Maybe not the last twenty years? Not long before then, though?'"

I gathered from his impression that the appraiser was not good with people. He knew antiques, but he couldn't let a man down easy when that man expected great things from his vase and had waited hours to be disappointed by it.

I imagined that most of the Roadshow appraisers weren't equipped to take harsh truths and soften them for the ones they told them to. They were like bad eulogists, one of which I'd heard that morning. It was my dad.

I took a long look at the vase. I said, "It's ceramic." I said, "It's from the late twentieth century, no doubt about that." That was more or less what the appraiser had said, but I made it sound a little better by using the word "century."

"I like what I see here," I said, and pointed to the mouth of the vase with the stirrer from my cocktail. I swept the stirrer up and down one of the vase's handles a couple of times and said, looking its owner in the eyes, "There's been some serious craftsmanship that's gone into this vase."

I asked him what "my colleague" had said it was worth and he said, "He told me it's worthless—and then he was like, 'It's worth nothing,' like he didn't just say that already." The man then put a toothpick in his mouth—I don't know where the toothpick came from.

I said, "Well, I can see where my colleague would get that impression, because vases from the 1980s—and I have no doubt this is one of them—tend to look similar. But if you'd be willing to lift this one so I can see its base—thank you. Yes! If you look here, this stamp indicates it's a product of the Sears group. Now, you might confuse the

31

Sears group with the Sears department store, but no: this Sears group was a team of artisans in Colorado who called themselves the Sears group on purpose. For them, it was something like a subversive act, putting the name of such a big, soulless company on what was, in fact, very soulful work.

"Sir," I said. "This vase is not worthless at all. I estimate its value somewhere between one and two hundred dollars."

Like the last guy, he was not overjoyed, but he was slightly happier than he'd been when he joined me. He carted his thing away silently, not thanking me or saying goodbye.

When I finished with my next customer, a woman with a wooden toy dog that I said was from the eighteenth century and probably worth $400, I looked up and discovered a line of a dozen tired-looking people had formed, half in polo shirts, all holding objects. I also discovered that my glass was empty, so as I lied to a sagging woman with a soapstone recreation of the skull of Frederick Douglass, saying it was "possibly worth thousands" and neglecting to tell her what a racist object I thought it was, the man in line behind her was kindly fetching me a refill.

It was my suit that had attracted these people, my black funeral suit and black tie. It wasn't that I looked good in the suit, which I did. It was that by wearing it I had inadvertently set myself apart from the people who'd brought their things to be appraised. The only others there who had dressed up were the appraisers, and I looked sharper than most of them, so everyone assumed I was there to appraise for the Roadshow.

I assured a small woman with a model rocking chair that it was "handcrafted" and "worth, at a conservative estimate, five thousand dollars." She believed me. It had to be the suit that made her believe me. I would have to start wearing it more often, I thought.

The more I drank, the higher my estimates of value climbed. I found that when I gave someone an unreasonably high appraisal, high enough to make his face turn red, he was likely to guffaw and offer to buy my "next round."

I did not turn these offers down. I didn't pay for another drink all afternoon.

I appraised a cuckoo clock and two normal clocks. I saw several objects made to hold poker chips. I saw an urn full of ashes, a sheep made of yarn, a Commodore 64, and a piece of metal that looked strangely familiar until I realized it was identical to the iron thing I'd been using to hold my toothbrush since I found it on the ground outside my apartment last year. I said it was from the 1930s, manufactured in Tulsa by "craftsmen" who have all died off, the secrets of their handiwork lost forever.

A theme of extinction ran through my late appraisals. I didn't intend it that way; I merely found, at one point, that the last five appraisals I'd given had stories attached to them in which at least two people died, usually many more. One involved what I called "a bad gun massacre."

I had long since transferred the marble frog from the inside pocket of my suit jacket to an outside pocket. I kept reaching in and rubbing it as I appraised, as if it were a talisman I kept for strength or luck.

The last artifact was brought to me by a woman about my mother's age. She had my mother's brown hair, tied like my mother's in a bun. I don't recall her face; the bun was more than enough for me. From a satchel she withdrew a drawing of the Eiffel Tower. She wore the most earnest expression I'd seen in hours as she asked me to tell her about it.

I took a long look, flipped it over, flipped it over again and said it was "drawn after the 1930s, naturally, since before then there was no Eiffel Tower." I smiled when I said this. She didn't smile back. Her non-smile turned to a frown when I said, "the penwork is admirable." She corrected me. It was a pencil drawing.

Maybe it was the booze—it was mostly the booze—but it was also that she looked like my mother: at that moment when she caught me in my lie, it felt like Mom had caught me lying again, like she had so many times, when I ate the marshmallows that were not meant for me, when I got caught sneaking out to get high with my girlfriend, when she found that I had taken away her cocaine and credit cards.

I couldn't look at the woman. I couldn't speak. I looked away and saw a man in a tie and a jacket, standing beside another table, watching me and mumbling into a cell phone. He was wearing a lanyard. This wasn't good.

I coughed into my hand—a genuine cough. I said, "Uh."

I felt my stomach climb up my throat.

I had one of those moments I sometimes have, in which I do something but as I'm doing it, I also see myself from the outside. Sometimes when I have these moments I am in the middle of a conversation and it throws me off, I forget what I was saying. What I saw myself doing this time was vomiting a day's worth of Old Fashioneds onto the drawing and the woman who was not my mom. I saw myself lunge, and try to get away, in an attempt to be anywhere other than at that table.

I saw a close-up of the carpeted floor as I landed there with my face on my arms and continued throwing up on my sleeves.

When I rolled over, face-up, the lanyarded man was standing over me. My hand was in my pocket, pawing the green marble frog. I was thinking, whatever happens next, I will not let them take this frog away.

The Man with the Nightmare Gun

I am not a serious man. I thought Carol understood this
about me by our fifth date. I thought it was something I'd
established the night of our third date, after we had sex the
first time. We lay together for an hour afterward, discussing
the vast range of bra sizes and the prehistoric giant sloth,
extinct now for thousands of years. It stood twenty feet tall
and had massive claws, Carol said. When she added that
people who lived when the sloths roamed the earth didn't
wear bras, I said, "They were the Greatest Generation."
    She laughed.
    Two dates later, I confessed to her my longstanding
fascination with guns. I thought she would understand that
I was only half-serious about this, though I was honest
when I speculated that guns were an interest American men
are conditioned for starting when we're toddlers. Guns
intrigued me for reasons I could not explain. I showed her
with my hands the size of what I imagined was the perfect
gun for me. I mimed pulling it from a shoulder holster and
aiming it at my calzone. I said, "Put the knife down, lady.
Drop that knife or I swear to God I'll drop you."
    Had I known how Carol would react to this, I never
would have done it. She was not amused, not in the least.
She leaned back in her chair, increasing her distance from
me and her spaghetti. The look she gave me was the look of
a woman who never wanted to see the man she was looking
at again. She would never let a gun into her house, she said.

In four and a half dates I had not upset her. Now I had. I thought I'd blown it, had taken a wrong turn and could not retrace my steps. This, I thought, was the end of date five.

Soon, though, my future wife pulled her chair back to the table. For the next five minutes she wouldn't look at me. She took a bite of her spaghetti from time to time. She gave me a series of insincere smiles, as if to let me know she knew I was still there. As if to remind me I was being ignored. We ate like someone had ordered us to finish our meals and we had to obey. I felt as if I'd been demoted. I paid the waiter and drove Carol home in silence.

When we arrived, she asked me to come inside.

I was only beginning to understand how Carol works. I had taken her silence to mean that all she wanted was to finish her spaghetti and never see me again. It didn't mean that. She merely wanted to get me to a private space so we could have a proper argument. Carol doesn't like public altercations. She doesn't like to make a scene, and I respect that.

Inside her apartment, she said she had almost been frightened of me when I spoke so passionately about deadly weapons. "I hate guns," she said in a way that made it clear that hers was not the passing disdain of the typical liberal arts school graduate. She had given it serious thought. She couldn't believe that this man she was falling in love with might want to divide his affections between her and a lethal weapon.

I had not known she was falling in love with me. I said I was sorry and meant it. I told her I knew better than to ever buy a gun. I would never take my interest in them that far. She nodded and said, "Good." Then we took each other's clothes off and forgot the whole thing.

I did my best, for Carol's sake, to put guns out of my mind. For several years after that night, other things occupied my mind—as Carol and I moved in together, as we got married, as we moved from our first house to a bigger house, and as Carol quit taking birth control after some long conversations about whether the time was right to have a child. We concluded that no time would be right to have a child, so we might as well do it before we got old.

Our lives settled. We were content with our jobs. We had a system that articulated which of us would make dinner each night of the week. I had Tuesdays, Thursdays and Sundays. We knew there would be no surprises in our lives, until the baby came and there would be nothing but surprises.

Then something changed. Or maybe nothing changed. Perhaps it was a matter of something I had buried reemerging, despite Carol. In the calm before the birth of our child, when my greatest worry was whether we had enough eggs to make quiche on a Sunday, Tuesday, or Thursday—if we didn't, I would have to go to Kroger and get more—I found that I was lacking something, something I could load bullets into, something with a trigger I could squeeze.

I wanted a gun in the old-fashioned sense of the word *want*. I didn't just desire a gun. I was lacking it, and its absence from my life was deeply felt. I wanted a gun with the same urgency our son would want Carol's breast when he was born.

I had no reason to own a gun. My friends didn't carry them. I didn't know how to shoot or clean one. I hadn't offended members of a local criminal organization. It simply seemed unthinkable that I lived in a country where I could so easily go out and buy a gun and I hadn't done so. There was also disbelief—that I had lived so long in a world that contained both me and guns and I'd never handled one. And I grew up in Kentucky.

~

One Saturday morning when Carol was at yoga, I went to Lion Pawn. For days I'd staked it out online. They had a black and yellow website, with big letters at the top that read WE BUY GOLD. Below that was a window with a short commercial full of sweeping shots of their inventory, followed by close-ups of excited children. The owner wanted his pawn shop to be a family-friendly establishment. He went so far as to flash the words FAMILY FRIENDLY across the screen.

I don't like to walk into buildings I've not been in before. When I do, I have the creeping sensation that everyone's eyes are on me. This was the case at Lion Pawn, where there was just one other person in the store. A bearded man in a hat stood behind the counter and said hello as I came in. I said, "Hi," and turned to the guitars, so as to seem less eager to reach the guns.

I had never been to a pawn shop. I was struck by how like a thrift store it was, but without the useless junk crowding the shelves. They had dozens of guitars and display cases of jewelry and guns—more of them than I'd expected. There were enough guns to arm a Boy Scout troop and make them into child soldiers. Behind the counter leaned a long row of shotguns, with a few assault rifles at one end. I could see them from where I stood among the guitars.

I didn't want to be with the guitars. I made my way through them, glancing at price tags so as to appear interested, but after a few minutes of fake browsing, I made my way to the handguns in a big, glass case. Some were little single-shot pistols. Others looked like flare guns, with fat barrels. I saw a .44 Magnum, and it was like seeing a celebrity in the flesh; there was no way not to notice it, and there was nothing else it could have been. It looked lethally heavy. It wasn't just any gun. It was a gun with a product line of huge condoms named after it.

Half the display case was reserved for semiautomatics, but I didn't want those. Berettas, Glocks—they're more machine than pistol. They look like they have something to hide. You can't see the bullets or where they go. They're stacked in the handle. I wanted something simpler, more naked. I wanted a revolver.

Made to greet the hand that grips it, the curves of a revolver are as smooth as young flesh. Its mechanism is ingenious. Pull the trigger and a bullet fires as the wheel turns to present another round. I have not had to study this design; thanks to TV and movies, it's as familiar to me as the recipe for scrambled eggs.

I was disappointed by the revolvers on display at Lion Pawn. I'd expected their metal parts to shine more brightly. I thought the wooden handles would look like they'd recently been Pledged. These guns looked used and worn, like they'd been fired too many times by men who never washed their hands.

But one revolver did stand out, even though it had the same faults. It was the simplest-looking gun, the one most like what I imagined when I pictured the perfect gun for me, my Platonic ideal. I pointed it out to the man behind the counter and said, "I'd like to see that one, please."

It was a Ruger Security Six. Its body was black steel, big letters on the barrel reading, STURM, RUGER & CO. INC. Its handle was wooden, with diamonds formed from divots etched on both sides. Above each diamond was a metal circle, half the size of a dime, bearing the image of an eagle. At first it looked like a phoenix—I mistook the broad feathers for flames—but when I looked closer, I found it wasn't burning. It was in flight.

Here was a pistol with character, one I could take home that day if I wanted. There are no laws where I live to slow such a transaction.

I paid the man his 500 dollars. He put my gun in a cardboard box. I bought a box of bullets—sixty for twenty dollars. I wouldn't have thought to get them, but the man asked, "You got ammo for that?"

Of course I didn't. I had not thought ahead to the projectiles I would shoot from my gun, why I would want to shoot them, or where they would go when I did.

All this took fifteen minutes. I spent another twenty walking home with the box in a plastic bag. I arrived before Carol and stowed the gun in the basement, in a desk my grandfather had kept in his shop before I was born. I don't have a shop. I have an office. My desk there is metal, and its drawers barely slide when you pull them. I would keep my gun in the sturdy desk of my father's father—not locked in a place where Carol couldn't reach it but where she wouldn't think to look in the first place.

The basement is a place that belongs to me, more or less. Carol goes there only for laundry purposes. In the years we've lived together, she hasn't touched the desk once.

I had a breakfast of toast and scrambled eggs ready by the time she arrived home. She would not know what I had done that morning. She would not see that I'd spent five hundred dollars at Lion Pawn with my debit card, because although we're married, we maintain separate bank accounts. Carol had other things on her mind, anyway. She was just beginning to show and was thinking more and more of the baby. She was reading *What to Expect When You're Expecting*, which I'd bought her after her last pregnancy test, remarking that soon I would need a different

book—*What Do You Expect Me To Do While You're Expecting?*
She had laughed at that.

She would not laugh if she knew what I had placed in the drawer of my grandfather's desk. She would scream at a rocket's pace to the nearest divorce lawyer.

~

I didn't touch the gun again that day. I had other things to do, and I wanted to spend time with Carol. Plus, I'd become a victim of buyer's remorse. I have made it sound as if my purchase of the gun was planned in advance. And I did plan it, in a way, over all those years I considered buying a gun. But I didn't leave the house that morning expecting to return with a pistol. I just did.

Now that I'd gone through with the purchase, I thought it might have been wise if I'd kept my desire for a gun in check. I'd spent five hundred dollars on something I didn't need.

I was couch-bound that afternoon, reading things online. I visited a site that was nothing but one page of nearly unreadable text—white words on a black background. I found it by searching the phrase, "Should I buy a gun?" The question was irrelevant, as of that morning, but I asked anyway.

The site was addressed to anyone who thought he should own a gun but wasn't convinced it was right for him. It was written for the man I had been just hours before. It started like this:

Before you buy a gun the first thing is to look in yourself and ask, is a gun the right for me? If a bad guy threatens me and/or my family can I bring myself to pull the trigger and risk killing him/her? Will I live with myself after the taking someone's life not with a knife but with a bullet?

I failed to see why it would be easier to live with stabbing a man than shooting him. A gun would be louder, yes, but if anything, I thought it would be far worse to stab someone and get covered with his/her blood than it would be to shoot an assailant from a distance, even a near distance. Yes, I thought, I could live with myself under these circumstances. I continued reading:

One of the most talked about but misunderstood part of the Bill of Rights is the Second Amendment. The Second Amendment is responsible for protecting many Americans from trouble, hostility and danger. Scholars have even said Amendment One and Two will change place, for freedom to speak will always turn to the gun for its defense.

Part of that was true, I thought. The second amendment was misunderstood. To Carol and so many others, Amendment Number Two exists for the sole purpose of arming and boosting the confidence of rednecks. It's something they associate with drunken hunters, murderers, and Charlton Heston. I'd been inclined to see it that way, too, in my pre-pistol years.

Now things were different. Now I was a man with a gun in his house. And while I wasn't about to join the NRA or visit their website, I was exercising a right I'd never given a workout before. I had owned deadly things all my life— kitchen knives, cars, blunt objects heavy enough for murder—but they didn't have amendments devoted to them. Of all my possessions, my gun was the only one our Founding Fathers had arranged for me to have the right to possess.

I shut my laptop and joined Carol upstairs. I placed my hand on her belly and gave her a husband's kiss. I didn't want to hold the gun that morning. I wanted to hold Carol.

~

Just before I bought my gun, I'd started to feel that
whenever I entered a room I would not be able to leave it.
"I don't mean this literally," I told Dale, my therapist, two
weeks before I entered Lion Pawn. "I don't think an
earthquake will level Kroger when I'm there and trap me
under the wreckage." It was worse than that, I said. Certain
places, certain rooms, were haunting me.

"But places," he said, "don't haunt people."

"Then forget the word *haunting*," I said. It was like I
could still feel a room inhabiting me after I walked out its
door. There were certain situations—dinners with friends of
Carol's, for example, friends who make no effort to hide
that they want to sleep with her despite how married we are
and how pregnant with my child she is—that I could not
shake off. I would replay these evenings for myself and
picture Carol's friend arranging herself as we entered the
restaurant, so that she would sit beside Carol, leaving me at
the far end of our table of eight. I watched her swill wine,
put her hand on Carol's arm, and lean against her
practically the whole time we were there.

And it wasn't just that. There was more to this than mere
jealousy. There were other places I could still feel inside me.
Like Kroger. When I stopped there on my way home from
work one Wednesday, I'd had a bad interaction with a
cashier regarding the accuracy of his scale. Our encounter
ended with my hands shaking and everyone watching me
sulk through the automatic doors. I couldn't return to
Kroger for a month, I was so humiliated. And I couldn't tell
Carol, because she would not understand.

Dale taught me a breathing exercise. Inhale for six
seconds, hold for six, exhale for another six. But I couldn't

45

do that constantly. I couldn't breathe like that when I was out walking.

~

For a long time, the gun did not leave the basement. There was nowhere I wanted to take it, nothing I wanted to shoot. I loaded it often, but only for the sake of doing it. I would stand six bullets in a row on the desk and slide them into their chambers, one by one.

Something guns have going for them is that they are sleek, metal objects. Other notable manufactured items have benefited from this status, Zippo lighters and pocket flasks among them.

My grandfather had a flask. It's small but holds just enough to get its user drunk. His initials—JHC—are engraved on its front. I keep it in my desk, full of whiskey, but I never take it with me out in the world. That would be the surest sign of a problem. I don't want to carry a metal container full of the very thing that killed the man who owned it before me. I want to live long enough to see my child grow old.

No one carries anything metal anymore. All accessories for men are now plastic, like my phone and my most recent pre-revolver acquisition, an Amazon Kindle.

On my Kindle I was reading *The Road*, by Cormac McCarthy, a book my friend Jamey recommended. I thought it might enhance my reading experience to hold the gun in one hand and the Kindle in the other as I thumbed through electronic pages. I suppose there's something about the feel of a pistol that makes despairing prose go down easier. When Carol wasn't home, I would go to the basement and sit in my chair, my feet on the desk, and hold the unloaded pistol, clicking the hammer back and pulling the trigger with an informal rhythm.

I did not do the things you might expect a man in his basement to do with a gun. When news came of the death of Osama bin Laden—just one week after I brought the gun home—I didn't hold it aloft, or point it at the wall, picturing him there and wishing I could have been the one to pull the trigger that ended his life. I didn't imagine the gun's barrel in Saddam Hussein's mouth as he begged for mercy. Nor did I picture making Qaddafi beg, or Putin.

My gun did not make me feel powerful. Many men seem to own guns for that purpose alone. They want to be grave threats and lack the patience for martial arts training. On message boards, they post footage of themselves at shooting ranges.

When I held my gun, I felt endangered, not dangerous. I was humbled. I knew what my gun could let me do, the swift end it could bring to my life and Carol's status as a married woman. There was fear in my fascination with the gun, but unlike other fears, like my fears of heights and spiders, it pulled me closer to its object.

I put the gun in my mouth on only one occasion. It was cold. It tasted, predictably, like metal. I held it there for a few seconds, then pulled it out. I put it back in my mouth a few more seconds and put it down, its barrel wet. I hadn't bought the gun for suicide purposes—I could not do that to Carol. I merely wanted to experiment, and now the experiment was over.

~

The next time I saw my therapist, I told him I'd bought the gun. He was dumbfounded. He said, "What possessed you to do that?"

The question irked me. I didn't want to list reasons. I wanted to discuss my latest enthusiasm. "I've always been interested in guns," I said. "I didn't grow up around them, but I knew people who did. So they've never been that foreign to me."

"But Carol doesn't want you to have one. Right?"

"Carol doesn't know about it."

"You've hidden it from her?"

"If she wanted to find it, she could."

"Mark."

What followed was a long effort to get to the bottom of what it was that had led me to spend so much money on something so hazardous to my life with Carol, and to life in general. He dug through several layers of explanation, each of which was sufficient for me, but not for him.

"I think it has something to do with jealousy," I told him. "I think I've always felt resentful because Carol has the Clitoral Hulk."

Carol had spent the last three years on our local roller derby team. The Clitoral Hulk was her alias. She'd wanted to call herself The Clitoral Hoodlum, but that name was taken by someone in California. There's an online database of alter egos of all the roller derby team members in America, created so that no one uses a name that's already in use. When I learned about that practice, it seemed polite and ladylike to me, even if it led some women to choose aliases like Carol's.

The way Carol talked about the Clitoral Hulk among friends made it sound like she had a secret identity. She would refer to the Hulk as if she were another person, as if it weren't just Carol wearing roller skates and a homemade uniform. "I wanted something like that," I told Dale. "I wanted something to identify with that no one would expect."

Dale wouldn't take that for an answer. We plodded on. I tried to tell him about the beauty I see in the design of a good pistol, but he shook his head and frowned, looking at me like I was a stranger he'd rather not know. He looked at me like Carol had looked at me the night of our fifth date. For a second I thought he was doing an unannounced kind of role-playing, in which he played Carol and I played myself.

I told Dale I was sorry. "Sorry?" he said, looking more disgusted. "I am not the one to whom you owe an apology." He was as appalled as Carol would be if she found my gun.

"I want you to get rid of the gun," he said. "Take it back where you found it. Do the right thing, do it tonight, and come back to see me next week."

~

I called Jamey and invited him out for drinks. I was holding my gun when I called him.

At the bar, he asked how Carol was doing. I asked after his pregnant wife. I didn't tell him I had bought a gun. Unlike Dale, he was not obliged to keep my secrets from Carol, so I brought up gun ownership as a hypothetical proposition. I said, "Is there anything that would make you want to buy a gun?"

He looked away for a few long seconds. Thinking. Sometimes he gets a look in his eyes that means he's got something good to say. He gazed at the bottles behind the bar, and said, "That's complicated. The way I see it—I don't know." He paused again, and said, nodding, "You could put all that money, all that manpower, into making anything." He took a deep breath and scratched his nose. "When you manufacture something, when you produce a thing that wasn't in the world before, you change the world. You can make an Elmo doll or a vibrator—those won't harm anybody. But when you bring a gun into the world, something that's made to do one thing, which is hurt people, you make the world more violent. More dangerous. You make it less likely that a person will make it safely from point A to point B."

He leaned aside and looked sidelong into my eyes.

I didn't tell him he was wrong. I didn't point out that a gun was just a thing, that its role in the world was determined by its owner. That you could own a gun and no one could die from it, and that happened all the time.

I didn't say that, actually, you could kill someone with a vibrator or an Elmo doll. A human being could choke on anything.

Sometimes a gun is not a weapon, I didn't argue. Sometimes it's just a gun.

Instead, "I'm with you," I said.

~

A few nights later I invited Craig to the same bar. Craig is different from Jamey—taller, for one, and with a beard. He doesn't orate the way Jamey will. Even though Craig is from rural Tennessee and I grew up in an upper-middle class part of Lexington, and no one believes I'm from Kentucky when I tell them because I never took on the accent, I've always felt a certain kinship with him that I never felt with Jamey, who's from Vermont.

To my surprise, I didn't even have to introduce guns into my conversation with Craig. He brought them up himself. He told me about a man at his store who had come in looking for shotguns. "That's not a problem, usually," he said. "But this man had on a shirt that said, 'Fuck that bitch,' and had this crazy look in his eyes. Something was wrong with his ears, too. I wanted to sell him some shampoo. I had to explain to him that we can refuse service to whoever we want, whenever we want, and we were refusing service to him. He did not take that lying down.

"He said, 'You kidding me?' He said, 'You know I can just go across town and get this same thing at another store.'" Craig shook his head.

"And then what?"

"I asked him what he thought he was going to do with his shotgun then. He said, 'What do you think I'm gonna do with it?' I said, 'I don't want to say what I think.' He laughed at that. He said, 'Listen, either you're gonna let me pay for this or else you're gonna pay for not letting me.' And that was it. I said, '*Out.*'

"He just walked away, and I was like, Asshole, you think I don't hear this shit all the time?"

"Wait. You do?"

"Yes, Mark. Every day. Not usually like that. But you wouldn't believe the guys who come in to buy a gun. Normal people do it, but there are plenty of guys who look like they just wandered in off the street, like they were out for a stroll and just decided to buy a gun, and it's like, who knows what they're gonna do with it. Sit in their kitchen and start making a list, maybe."

I said, "I'd buy a gun if I was allowed to."

"You say that," he said. "But I don't think it's true."

"I mean it," I said, and I told Craig what I'd been wanting to tell someone since I bought the gun. I told him about wanting a revolver, rather than any other sort of gun.

"And it has everything to do with that word—*revolver*," I said. I went on to explain that *revolver* was a near-perfect word. Almost, but not quite a palindrome, it evokes, in its movement, the smooth rotation of the gun's cylinder from one chamber to the next.

I thought Craig would be sympathetic to this. He probably says *revolver* several times a day. But he looked down at the bar. "Mark," he asked. "What makes you think you should have a gun?"

I explained that I've never been an especially handy guy, that I didn't grow up with a hands-on father, which I thought he'd understand, since he grew up without any father. No one taught him to fix a broken door or change a tire, and I never learned to do those things either.

I told him that when I'd bought a house with Carol, I thought I'd learn to patch a leaky pipe and replace a hinge. But it didn't work out that way. Most of the time I'm busy at my job. There's no need for me to fix things. If a pipe breaks, we call a man who comes from a long line of hands-on dads and pay him to come fix it for us. In fact, whenever I suggest fixing something on my own, Carol calls one of those well-fathered men instead, someone who knows what he's doing.

A gun, I told Craig, is a small thing that demands maintenance, a metal thing I could learn to take apart, reassemble, and clean. One reason to own a gun, I said, would be to learn how to really use something. "I can't do that with my Kindle."

Craig laughed, and for a second that was all he did. Then he said, "Well, I guess you do need a gun then," and he laughed some more as he returned his attention to his beer.

~

One night, a few weeks later, when Carol was asleep with our baby inside her, I went to the basement and withdrew the gun and flask from the desk. I took a long drink and laid the flask before me. At two in the morning, I beheld three objects from my chair—flask, gun, Kindle. I thought the whiskey would make me tired, but as the moments passed my insomnia went unabated.

If my grandfather's flask had his initials on it, I thought, then the gun I'd chosen as my hand-held ornament should say something more than STURM, RUGER & CO. INC. I wanted to make a mark on this thing for whichever person found it when I was dead or in enough of a coma to make Carol give up hope. When I can't speak for myself, I thought, I'll want to speak through this pistol. I'll want everyone to know it was mine.

My father had given me a file as one piece in a tool set that served as a housewarming present. I said to Carol at the time that I could take his gift in one of two ways—a passive-aggressive acknowledgment of how he'd never taught me to use tools, or an apology for the same. At the desk, underground, I used that file on my gun, like a convict scratching at his bars, as if I were attempting to break out of something and into the barrel of the gun.

I tried to write my name across one side of the barrel, but when I got to the letter K, I made a mistake. Somehow the K looked more like an E, with one horizontal bar missing. It looked like I had started to write MARE, but my arm had gotten tired and I'd stopped filing.

I couldn't fix it. And I wasn't about to return to Lion Pawn and buy a new pistol. I thought for a minute and did the only thing I could think of. I finished the E and—very carefully now—extended the word, as if playing a game of gun-Scrabble.

When I finished, it read NIGHTMARE.

It wasn't what I wanted, but it was better than MARE.

~

The next night I lay awake in bed, beside Carol, past midnight, attempting again to sleep. At one-thirty, I went to the basement and sat at my grandfather's desk. I pulled the gun from its drawer. It said NIGHTMARE, but it was a word that was irrelevant to both the gun and its owner. I sipped whiskey from my grandfather's flask. I would not risk botching another word. One side of the barrel read NIGHTMARE. The other side would have a series of notches up and down its length. It would be simple, I thought. It would be enigmatic. I went to work marking the gun's barrel.

When I finished, it looked like this: / / / / / / / / / /.

It looked as if I'd made each mark after using the gun to kill someone. I put the file away. I put the gun in its drawer. I returned to my bed and didn't sleep until four in the morning.

~

The next night, I took my insomnia to the basement again, but this time I brought my shoes and clothes. Carol didn't stir. This would be, I decided, the first night I took my gun outside. I would creep out through the basement window. Carol wouldn't hear me leave from up in our room. If she woke when I returned to our bed, I would tell her I'd spent those hours downstairs with my Kindle.

In my jeans and jacket I walked our little town's streets, the gun buried in my pocket, in my hand. I didn't fire it. I didn't want to get arrested. I didn't want anything. I was just walking. The gun wasn't even loaded.

Two nights later, though, I took another late walk, and before I ventured out, I loaded all six chambers. I had no plans to shoot anything or anyone or to do anything in particular. I just thought as long as I had the gun, it might as well be full of ammunition.

~

The next time I saw Dale, I told him I'd taken my gun back to the pawn shop.

He told me he was proud of me, that I had done the right thing. I shouldn't tell Carol, he went on. It would only hurt her, and if she didn't know about it, no harm done. After a long sigh—Dale sighs often—he said I needed a mantra.

That wasn't what he called it; he called it an "affirmation," but I had prior associations with that word and didn't want it to apply to anything that came out of my mouth.

He told me his mantra had helped him find a partner. Whenever he started to doubt himself in his long hunt for a good man in our small town, he had said to himself, "I deserve to be with the perfect man for me." He repeated these words many times a day. A few months later, he was with Jon, with whom he has lived for the last seven years.

I liked his mantra. It was simple. It wasn't for me, though. I had to come up with my own. Dale asked what I'd like mine to be. For a moment I thought he expected me to have my mantra figured out in a few seconds, but he told me I should think about it and tell him what I came up with when I returned.

All the rest of that day I tried out mantras in my head. *I deserve to be with the perfect man. I am the perfect man for Carol. I am the perfect man.* I decided I should lose the "perfect man" foundation of Dale's mantra and make mine more specific to my needs. *I am the man that I have chosen to be*, I went on. *I am what I have chosen to be. I am where I have chosen to be.*

55

I am in the room where I have chosen to be.
I am in one room and there I have chosen to be.
I will leave when I decide to leave.
When I decide to leave, I will have left.
All the rest of that day, I recited mantras in my head.
They continued to change, as if on their own, each one
becoming the next without my influence.

~

When Carol and I first moved to this suburb, we were
amazed at how quiet it was at night. Before we moved here,
we'd lived not far from Cleveland's city center, where there
was constant noise out our window. At one a.m., at three,
at four, we heard dogs barking, distant trucks, people
shouting. Out here, there is almost no noise at all, as if
silence is something sacred to us and our neighbors,
something we've agreed should never be disturbed.

Given that, one might expect a gunshot to make a
stronger impression than mine seemed to make on my sixth
walk with my gun, when I finally fired it. Despite the crack
of the pistol and the flash, there were no consequence for
what I did. I heard no sirens. Granted, the place I fired it
was a footpath where no one seems to walk, especially at
night. And the sound of the pistol wasn't nearly as loud as I
thought it would be.

I hadn't seen the fawn until we were very near one
another. She scared me. I was trudging through the poorly
lit path when I glanced aside and caught sight of her head,
just six feet from where I froze. I thought she was a dog. I
thought she was a pit bull poised to kill me. Her nose was
tilted to one side. Her eye was on me. I don't recall raising
the gun, which was already in my hand. I remember firing. I

recall how hard I had to squeeze the trigger to make the gun go off.

When I fired, the barrel dropped a bit. I missed her head. I don't know where I hit her, but as I turned to run, I heard her wheeze. I didn't think a deer could wheeze, not the way this one did. She sounded like a person, like a deathbed respirator. She exhaled only once before I ran as fast as I could run.

I was tempted to drop the gun but didn't. I held it tightly all the way home. My heart was still pounding when I rejoined Carol in bed. I did not sleep that night.

~

All the next day, and the day after that, I checked the local paper online, at ten-minute intervals, for signs that someone had reported the gunshot or the wounded deer I'd left in the path. Nothing came up. Perhaps the police were keeping it quiet, or maybe dead deer don't get reported in the paper. I don't know. I didn't want to know.

I kept the gun in the desk for days, convinced I should get rid of it. I couldn't return it to the pawn shop, though. What if the police had warned them to watch for a gun like the one used on the baby deer? What would they make of the inscription I'd made?

I might have thrown it away, had I known where to throw it, but gradually I began to calm down.

I have not fired it since and not because I haven't had more night encounters with young mammals. I have had to think hard about what my gun means to me. I have weighed what it was made to be against what it has the potential to be.

The gun does not have to be a weapon. Like my grandfather's flask, it can be a kind of emblem.

57

When I am dead, someone will find my gun. Whoever it is will not know about the deer or what I did in this basement when I still lived, but the gun will make a bold impression—certainly bolder than the Kindle's. It will be a sign that the people in my life did not really know me. It will tell its discoverer that there was more to me than they thought there was, that something in me defied recognition in all those years I spent aboveground.

~

I do not give up on my ever-changing mantra. I recite it through the fights I have with Carol that start when she asks why I am so distracted. I repeat it through our frantic drive to the hospital. I whisper it under my breath as I hold my son for the first time and an anaesthetized Carol dozes off.

I am in one room and there I am.
I am in a perfect room.
I keep a perfect gun in a perfect room.
My gun is a perfect room.
I am nowhere but where I am.

I think my gun is my mantra. It makes a plain statement, an affirmation so simple, so perfect, it need not be repeated.

And when I am dead, it will belong to my son. He'll open the bottom drawer of his great-grandfather's desk to find a piece of me left intact, a piece he never knew, my pistol, my mantra, and it will be as if he's hearing my voice for the first time.

The Vinyl Canal

It started with *1999*. Ben scratched his copy when he dropped it on his bathroom floor. I don't know why he took *1999* into the bathroom. He said the scratch ruined "Let's Pretend We're Married," took the third minute "out at the knees." The song didn't repeat itself, like on a classic broken record. It stumbled over the best parts, skipping across where Prince says, "C'mon baby, let's ball."

Ben didn't like that. *1999* wasn't his favorite record, he made sure to tell me, but this new damage mattered. He thought if a song didn't work, he ought to bypass it completely.

"I've never pretended I was married," I said. "Not to anyone." I wanted to see what Ben would say to that.

He said, "You can't skip a song on a record, like you can with a CD—it's the one advantage a CD has over a record."

I didn't care about the CD advantage, and I didn't know why I was talking to Ben. I usually avoid guys like him, who never smile, who don't walk so much as plunge forward, who I can't picture, for the life of me, anywhere in ten years. He had a moustache, which I like to keep my distance from, and he was the sort of person who doesn't seem to be aware that there are other people around, even when he's talking to them.

I don't know why I still live in a town full of guys like Ben. Maybe every town is full of them.

Three years ago, I graduated from college, the same college that's responsible for keeping our little town on life support. Instead of leaving when I graduated, like I thought I would, I got a job at the Amazon warehouse, and when I'm not working there, I'm usually drinking coffee. It's how I end up talking to guys like Ben.

I knew him just well enough to drink coffee with him at Prague's, the coffeehouse where we ran into each other. He used to be a friend of a friend, but that's not what he was anymore. I didn't know what he was anymore, except Ben.

He said, "I took an X-Acto knife and etched a gash into the first track of side two of record one of *1999*."

"You etched a gash."

"I don't like to think of it as a gash," he said. "It's more like I was installing an elevator, something to take me not along each individual groove to the record's middle, but on one long groove, and fast. Like a canal."

I asked Ben what it sounded like. He said the way it went through the song was jerky. The record just sounded broken. "It doesn't matter," he said. "I didn't like that song much."

Ben was someone who could not determine when the person he was talking to was less interested in what he was talking about than he was. "I watched the way the needle moved along the canal," he said. "I saw that when I dug the next one, I would need to be more of an artisan with the X-Acto. I'd have to make the canal curve, rather than plow through the song in a straight line. If I wanted a smoother transition, I mean."

"And you did."

"I thought I could do it without sacrificing speed, without adding more than a second to a record's total playtime—adjusting for the whole song I took out of it."

It was Ben's good fortune to have an extra copy of Blue Öyster Cult's *Agents of Fortune* at his apartment. He'd found it in a dollar bin in Columbus some months prior, he said, and bought it because it didn't seem right to leave a good copy in the dollar bin.

"But when I listened to the new copy," he said, "I found that the second song on side one, 'True Confessions,' was beyond choppy. It was unlistenable. So I painted with Wite-Out what I thought would be a gradual passage through the broken song.

"I knew I was violating the artists' intentions. But this was important."

Ben etched a canal into *Agents of Fortune*, as he had with *1999*. He sat back in his desk chair and listened to his work, or his and Blue Öyster Cult's work. "It sounded good," he said. "There was static, but it was like there had never been 'True Confessions.'" He listened all the way to the part just before "The Revenge of Vera Gemini," where Patti Smith reads a poem.

"Patti Smith?" I said.

"Yeah. She used to go out with Allen Lanier."

"Who's Allen Lanier?"

"He was in Blue Öyster Cult."

It wasn't surprising that I didn't know this. I like Patti Smith. She's one of the women of rock 'n' roll. But I didn't like her enough to have memorized her relationship history.

Ben said he liked her, too, but he didn't like the poem she read on *Agents of Fortune*. He said he tried digging a canal through the poem, into the beginning of the song. He said it worked pretty well. "It got me thinking," he said, "that there are probably no more than fifty albums that are perfect all the way through. Albums that, when I hear them, don't make me want to rush through any of the songs. *What's Going On* is one of them. So is *So*."

61

"Oh," I said. "So is *Vespertine*."

"What?"

"Björk. *Black on Both Sides* is perfect."

"So is *Sabotage*. The Black Sabbath one, I mean."

"A lot of David Bowie albums are perfect."

Ben narrowed his eyes. "I don't know. *Station to Station*, maybe."

"*White Light White Heat*."

"Yeah, anyway."

"Right."

"It got me thinking. I've got just over 670 records, and at least 600 of them have parts I don't like listening to. So I went to Ace Hardware for some better etching supplies. I didn't tell them what I was etching. I went home and took 'Fluff' out of *Sabbath Bloody Sabbath*."

"I didn't know that had fluff," I said.

"The song's called 'Fluff.' I took 'A Man Needs a Maid' out of *Harvest* and 'The Weight' from *Music from Big Pink*."

"Isn't that the song people like?"

"I've heard it so many times," said Ben. "It doesn't sound good to me anymore. And I said *So* is a perfect album, but it shed seven pounds when I removed 'We Do What We're Told.'"

Why *seven* pounds? I wondered.

Ben also dug a canal, he said, that started at the middle of a song on *Wish You Were Here* and ended somewhere in the middle of the next song. "When I listened to it again, I couldn't even tell there was a canal there. Fucking Pink Floyd," he said. "I haven't gotten around to it yet, but I want to dig a canal from the start to the end of both sides of Bob Dylan's *Shot of Love*."

"Wow."

"It'd be a much better record."

"I didn't touch *The Low End Theory*, though," Ben added, seeming to want to reassure me. "I didn't touch *How I Got Over* or *Return to Cookie Mountain*."

I didn't know what he was talking about anymore.

We were silent, and it was uncomfortable. There were a lot of people around, mostly our age, and they were working on things on their computers.

Ben said he kept thinking about the Vinyl Canal.

"It's not just made of vinyl," he said. "It's not just what I did to certain records to make them more listenable. It's all around us. It preceded us by thousands of years."

Ben went to get a refill. I considered leaving, to avoid hearing what he would say next. I'd spent enough of my life listening to weird men talk about things that matter to them but that don't really matter at all.

How much more of my life would I spend doing that— sitting patiently while someone like Ben told me all about something that really meant something—to him?

How much longer would it be before I had a man living inside my head, droning on about records, or traffic, or the independent comedy scene, or the independent literature scene, or the independent scenery scene, whenever there wasn't a real man around to do it? How long before I had a man living in my apartment, who would serve the same purpose?

I could have just left. But I wasn't done with my coffee, and it had cost three dollars. And I was supposed to meet my friend Megan there in less than ten minutes. So, whatever.

When Ben returned, he said, "It got me thinking, about how the Vinyl Canal is more than just what I did with my records. It's bigger than that. It's whenever someone tries to bypass something he doesn't want to face."

"Isn't that a shortcut?"

"No," he said. "A shortcut's already there. You don't make it, you take it.

"The Vinyl Canal is when you go out of your way to try to make something easier, but instead you cause yourself a lot more trouble than you would have had if you'd left it alone. It's like when the legislature cut funding to the library, so it wouldn't stay open hardly at all, and the people couldn't make themselves smarter. They cut the hours to keep everybody stupid. It must have been hard work to make that happen. There must have been arguments, with library people pushing back."

"You mean librarians?"

"Yeah, and library customers."

"Patrons?"

"It was a way to make people stagnate, and they didn't have to poison any reservoirs. They did it by digging a canal through things that were important to people, the way I dug a canal through 'Nearly Midnight, Honolulu,' on Neko Case's *The Worse Things Get, The Harder I Fight, The Harder I Fight, The More I Love You*."

"You should have dug a canal through that long-ass album title."

"Or the way they diverted the water supply in Flint, Michigan, and poisoned all those children. That was the Vinyl Canal. And it was the Vinyl Canal when the Bush administration promoted intelligence, they knew was faulty to justify invading Iraq."

I wanted to tell Ben to slow down. His face and voice had grown red and intense. He seemed to be out of breath when he slurped his coffee. It was like he was trying to dig a canal through the table with his words.

"The Vinyl Canal," he said, leaning forward, "was the tape they put over the lock to the Democratic Party headquarters at the Watergate Hotel. It was when they erased the tape from Richard Nixon's Oval Office recordings. And it's shock therapy, too."

"Shock therapy?"

"It takes a lot of work to shock the shit out of somebody's mind. It causes so much pain and makes you need more treatment later that maybe actually works."

Surely, I thought, Ben was not a victim of shock therapy.

He was quiet now, looking not at me but above my head, at an amateur portrait of Joan Crawford.

"I guess," I said, "the Vinyl Canal was my parents staying together for the sake of their kids, instead of getting divorced."

Ben nodded.

"It was supposed to make our lives easier. It meant a lot more work for them, though. And I fucking hated it."

"That sounds about right," said Ben. "And it was when Jane left me, because she thought it'd be easier to do that than to try to make things work."

Oh, boy.

"I don't mean," said Ben, "to compare Jane leaving me with the war in Iraq. She had much better reasons to leave than the U.S. had to invade Iraq.

"She didn't like how much money I spent on records. That was fair. I don't spend *that* much on them, but if you don't like records it seems like a lot."

"If Saddam Hussein had spent too much money on records," I said, "that would have been a better reason to invade Iraq than the reasons we had for going in."

"Oh," said Ben. "I forgot to mention I dug a canal through 'Beside You,' on *Astral Weeks*."

I was looking at a woman at another table I'd made out with once, when Ben said, "Wait a minute. The police. That's a big one."

"*Zenyatta Mondatta*?"

"What?"

"Did you want to canal that record?"

"Not those Police. The real police."

"Not the Dream Police?"

Ben looked around and looked back at me. "Please don't tell anyone about this," he said.

"About what?"

"Just don't. Please."

"Who would I tell?"

"I don't want anyone else to take credit for discovering this."

Holy shit, I thought.

"I have to go," he said.

And he went.

~

When Megan arrived, we talked about Ben. I hadn't seen Megan in a while, and I didn't really want to talk about Ben, but he had just spent fifteen minutes telling me about something that made no sense.

"That guy's weird," Megan said.

"I know," I said.

"He's so twitchy," Megan said.

"And weird," I said.

I knew it was unfair, but I felt Megan ought to take some responsibility for how weird Ben was. Or, anyway, for my having had to be a part of his weird life for so long. She was the one who had introduced us, some months prior, at the same table where the woman I'd made out with was now sitting with another woman. She kept looking at me and smiling faintly—remembering, perhaps, and reminding me with her faint smile, how we had made out but then not talked about it or to each other since, which I thought was dumb. Maybe she thought it was dumb, too.

I'd never made out with a woman before she kissed me.

Megan knew Ben much better than I did, but she was acting like we were weirded out by him equally. It wasn't fair.

Still, when Ben contacted me via Facebook, a week later, to ask if I would join him on a local radio show to talk about the Vinyl Canal, I didn't want to say yes, at least not at first. But saying no didn't appeal to me, either.

Four hours after asking me to go on the radio with him, he wrote to ask again.

If someone other than Ben had done that, I would have thought he was trying to sleep with me, or kill me, but I knew Ben didn't want me for sex or murder. He was harmless. So I went.

~

The show was called *Here We Are Now*. It was a call-in show that ran from nine to midnight on Thursday nights at the college radio station. Callers would ask, mostly, what the host, D-Day, thought of things, like bands and current events. He would tell them what he thought. He played music, and there were theme nights. Sometimes he wanted people to call the show if they didn't have an appendix. One time, all the callers had to not have any brothers or sisters. It was the show I paid the most attention to because I don't have any brothers or sisters, except in the sense that we are all brothers and sisters.

I met Ben at the radio studio's lobby. There were a couch and a couple of chairs, and in the other room was D-Day, talking to our little college town about what was on his mind.

Ben was in one of the chairs when I arrived. He had some records with him. "You're ready for this, right?" he said.

"Yeah," I said, shrugging in my olive-green jacket, sensing that no matter how ready I was I would never be as ready as Ben was, for anything.

"You remember what I said about the Vinyl Canal?"

"Yes," I said.

"I just want to make sure we're on the same page."

"It's just a radio show," I said.

"And you're up to the challenge?"

"I used to be a DJ, Ben. This isn't a challenge."

"You were on *college* radio, though, right?"

"Ben," I said. "This is college radio."

"The Vinyl Canal," said Ben, once we were on the air, "is whenever someone makes a serious effort to make their lives easier, usually at the expense of other people, or a principle, but it ends up requiring more work to dig the canal than it would have been to leave things as they were, pre-canal."

"But you said this was something you were doing with your record collection," said D-Day.

"That's right. Like with *Astral Weeks*."

"What'd you do to that?"

"I dug 'Beside You' out of it. I made a groove right through the song that's just deep enough so the needle will travel past the song without playing it."

"Good call," said Caroline, D-Day's sidekick. She was nodding and taking a drink. "But," she said, "isn't the Vinyl Canal supposed to damage other people's lives? It sounds like you're damaging your own life. And your records."

"I'm not damaging them," said Ben. "Have you tried listening to *Songs of the Wood* in its entirety?"

"No."

"It's really terrible," I said. I had never heard *Songs of the Wood*. I didn't even know what band was responsible for *Songs of the Wood*. From the title, I thought it was probably Jethro Tull.

"But it doesn't have to be harmful to people, necessarily," said Ben. "The Vinyl Canal can be dug at the expense of a principle."

"How is what you're doing at the expense of a principle?"

"Okay. For starters, it's not what the artists who made the records intended. I've been violating their intentions, big time. But the important thing is that it takes a lot more work to carve lines into records than it does to listen to the parts of them you don't like."

"And that's why it's the Vinyl Canal."

"Exactly."

I took a drink of water. Caroline nodded and looked at me with her lips pursed.

"The thing with the records, though," said Ben, "is small-time. It's really nothing, compared to what the police are doing, day in and day out."

"I didn't know they got back together."

"Not those Police," Ben said. "Police officers. They violate people's rights constantly, for the sake of expediency, to make their jobs easier."

"That's a pretty big leap, isn't it?" said D-Day, who was right about it being a leap. "To go from *Astral Weeks* to police harassment?"

"You seem to be taking this seriously," said Caroline.

"I am," said Ben. "I do." None of the listeners could see how serious he looked, but D-Day and Caroline could. I watched Caroline glance at D-Day, then look at Ben, and I thought, Oh, no.

"Why are you so worked up about this?" said Caroline, and the way she said it told me that she meant to put herself at a substantial distance from Ben and his enthusiasm. Which was fair. But I could also sense that she was about to start making Ben sound like a freak.

Which he was. But still.

"I'm actually pretty amped about it, myself," I said.

I wasn't supposed to be talking. When I was introduced, Ben had interjected that I was "just along for the ride," and as soon as I spoke, he frowned at me.

I said, "My own Vinyl Canal is online shopping."

"It is?" said D-Day.

"I shop for clothes and things online to save myself the trouble of going to the store. But the images of the clothes are so small. I can't see what they really look like. I can't touch them. I end up going to a store, after all. It's a waste of time."

Caroline took a big drink of whatever she was drinking out of her Klean Kanteen. I wished it were poison.

"That's a really good example," said Ben, when no one else said anything.

"Okay," said D-Day. "So it's like when Obama wanted to make healthcare more accessible, but instead of going single-payer he engineered a convoluted thing that's not as good for people."

"Yeah," I said.

"Sure," said Ben.

I have moments when I'm not certain if I am or am not having racist thoughts. When D-Day criticized Obama, I felt weird about it, because D-Day is black, and I couldn't help thinking, just for a second, that it was messed up for him as a black man to criticize our first black president.

Of course, D-Day can say what he wants. He's not betraying anyone. It isn't good that I think things like that.

I don't think it was a microaggression, though, because I kept it inside.

~

The first caller was a young-sounding man who told D-Day he'd been too soft in a previous show on the issue of space tourism. "Don't you think it's a real problem?" he said. D-Day rolled his eyes at Caroline as the young man said they were filling space with space junk, and that every ship that orbited Earth for recreation left manufactured debris that had no business being there. D-Day said, "Space has a whole lot more debris in it already than what the tourists are leaving up there. It's called planets."

Ben nodded vigorously.

The next caller seemed to have paid attention to the conversation we'd been broadcasting. "It sounds to me," she said, "that what you're talking about is a lifehack."

"It does sound like that," said Caroline, smiling at Ben with the corners of her mouth. Or its edges, maybe. Mouths don't have corners.

"This is different from a lifehack," said Ben. "A lifehack makes your life easier. This makes it more complicated. It's the Vinyl Canal."

The next caller had a different problem. I don't know how to describe his voice, or any voice, really. All I can say is he sounded large and angry.

"I want to address something the second lady said," he said.

"Do you mean me?" said Caroline.

"No," he said. "The other girl. Who thinks online shopping is an inconvenience? I have never heard anything so ridiculous in my life."

There was a brief silence. "Okay," said D-Day, looking at me, as if to make sure I was okay.

I was fine.

"I don't see how anyone can say that," said the man on the phone.

Everyone was looking at me. "I don't really know what I can add to what I said already," I said.

"If you have such a problem with shopping online," the man said, "then why don't you not do it? Why not just not do it and let other people enjoy their lives?"

I said, "I didn't say anything about other people not enjoying life."

"That's a good thing. I intend to keep shopping online, because I find it's very convenient. I am in a wheelchair. Many stores in this area choose not to accommodate me."

Had this been my show, I would have hung up on the man before he could say that and moved on.

"What kinds of things do you buy online?" asked Caroline.

"Shotgun shells."

"Thanks for the call," said D-Day.

The next caller was also angry but sounded like maybe he hadn't been angry for as long as the previous caller. Like he had only gotten angry that day. "It was that statement your guest read about online shopping," he said. I looked at Ben, but he wasn't looking at me. "I am tired," said the caller, "of people who want to badmouth and trash the internet but use it all the time for everything. The internet's brought us so many things. I think it's easy for some people to take it for granted."

"I didn't say anything about hating the internet," I said. "I just have trouble with shopping online sometimes. The images are too small. Especially on my phone."

The next caller asked what kind of clothes I'd been shopping for, and I told him, "Regular clothes." I didn't want to give him any personal information.

He said, "What I really wanted to call about was, you said something about the internet that was ridiculous. I think you said it was overrated? Microaggressions like that don't belong on a college radio station, which is funded by my tax dollars. I'll take my response off the air."

D-Day went immediately to a station identification.

During it, Ben put his hand over the mic in front of his face, which he didn't need to do, as it had been switched off for the moment, and said, "Do you think you could talk less?"

"Less?" I said. "I've barely said anything."

"I want to try to stay focused," said Ben, "on the Vinyl Canal."

~

D-Day came back from the station break and announced that we'd now hear one of Ben's records with the Vinyl Canal dug through it—*Let It Be*, by the Beatles.

Ben explained to me, as the song played, and Caroline and D-Day talked with one another without acknowledging us, which I thought was rude, that he'd taken "Let It Be" out of *Let It Be*. He told me why, but I didn't listen.

Nor did I listen to the songs. I browsed the selection of scarves at Scarves.net on my phone. One of the songs played, then there was static, and then another song played. I felt certain I'd heard both songs before, but I couldn't have said what they were. That's how I feel about nearly all songs by the Beatles.

Ben was grinning when D-Day resumed taking calls. He looked proud.

He wasn't grinning or looking proud when the next caller came on the air and said he couldn't believe what Ben had done to *Let It Be*. "How could you do that?" he said. "That's one of the classic songs."

Ben stammered. A radio Prometheus, he had not expected an outraged response to his great gift to the small town we lived in. He was stunned.

I wasn't stunned. I said, "Something I think we can all agree on is that when my friend Ben hears an overrated song, he will not let it be."

No one in the studio was amused.

I was amused, when the next caller called in to say that he thought what Ben had done was copyright violation.

"It is not," said Caroline. "I've been studying this in law school. The records are Ben's. He can do what he wants."

"It may not be what the artists intended," added Ben, "but I'm not reselling the records. That would be a problem."

The next caller wanted to talk more about what I'd said earlier about shopping. "I don't think that girl knows what she's talking about," said the man.

Is it the same man calling in, I wondered, pretending to be different men? What was going on?

D-Day hung up on that caller. He said, "I've got another vinyl canal. Smartphones. They're supposed to make life easier; they're supposed to help me get in touch with people. But I don't even use the phone to make calls. Just to get someone's attention, I go through Facebook."

"It's also like scraping ice off your windshield," said Caroline, "in the wintertime."

"How so?" asked D-Day, who looked intrigued.

"Yeah, how so?" asked a caller who I hadn't realized was on the line.

"Well," said Caroline, "you can just turn up the heat in your car and get warm yourself while the car warms up. The ice is gonna melt if you do that. You don't have to do all that scraping. It creates more work and wears your body out."

"I can see it," said D-Day, and I thought, they must be fucking. That's the only way he would agree with what she'd just said.

"It's also police violence," said Ben. "To get back to that."

Here it comes, I thought. The moment no one has been waiting for.

"The police need to keep us in our places," Ben said. "They need to keep their boots on our throats. But instead of doing it in a way that's slow or that means they need to get out of their cars and talk to people, walk a beat and get to know a neighborhood, they just shoot people. And Taser them, and beat them. And it ends up causing more problems in the long run, which isn't what the police intend. It's going to unite the public against them. People won't just take it forever."

Ben swallowed a couple of times. It was unclear if he was going to say more.

I saw how necessary it was that he not say more.

Maybe most police, nationwide, are great people who are just misunderstood. But the cops in our little town are a bunch of small-time fascists. They shot my friend Elizabeth with a Taser when all she had done wrong was ask why she got pulled over. They shot a guy's dog when they raided his house for drugs. It turned out to be the wrong house.

I've heard that some of our local cops are serial rapists.

Maybe they're not, but I felt I had to intervene on Ben's behalf, to save him from them, in case they were listening,

75

or in case they heard about what he'd said live on the radio and came seeking retribution.

I said, "The Vinyl Canal is also when I go out with guys and it turns out they hate women, like, all women altogether. But they don't do it in a straightforward way. Maybe they don't even know they hate women. They just say crappy things and act like they're in a porno half the time."

Ben had his hand on his face as I spoke.

I'd said what I said to save Ben, though to save him from—what? Police retaliation? Maybe. Definitely to save him from having to defend what he'd said to the radio trolls, who then called, one after another, not to tell Ben he was wrong about the police, but to say I was wrong to say what I had said, that men weren't really like that, or that not all men were, and anyway I should move to a different country if I didn't like the way things were.

It was all anyone wanted to talk about anymore. A man called in to say I should try going out with nice guys.

Like I didn't know better than to fall for that.

A woman called in to suggest I stop dating guys. I think it was the woman I'd made out with, the one I saw at Prague's. She may have recognized my voice on the air and decided to call in.

Another man called to say I should "look into getting [my] pussy stapled shut."

That was the end of Ben and my appearance on the radio, and I wondered if it was the end of D-Day's college radio career.

D-Day thanked us for being on his show and said we'd hear side A of *Dark Side of the Moon* as the show came to a close.

The only song the listeners heard was "Time." Ben had Vinyl-Canaled all the other songs, to make the record better.

Ben didn't take his eyes off the floor as we left the building. We didn't speak until we were out of there, but when we were, I asked Ben how he thought it had gone.

"I didn't like that Caroline," he said.

"I know," I said. "At first I felt bad for feeling like that. Then she said she was a law student, and I was like, I don't feel bad anymore."

"Well," said Ben.

"Right," I said.

"Why did you have to say that—about men?" said Ben. He looked hurt. Not like he was going to cry; not angry, just hurt.

I sighed. "I don't know," I said. "I guess I got carried away." I could have told him what kind of backlash I had probably saved him from. "But listen," I said. "People heard you. You got your message out. You got to say what you wanted to say. Right?"

"I guess I did," he said.

"I mean, I don't think it'll be the end of police violence."

"No. But it helps advance the conversation."

"Sure it does."

"Well," said Ben, looking away already. "See you later."

He was gone before I even said goodbye. It was Ben's way. He meant nothing by being so abrupt.

As I walked to my car, I texted Megan to ask if she thought there were always trolls or if they came into being thanks to the internet.

She said she didn't know.

On my drive home, I went through a residential neighborhood, to avoid downtown, where there was usually traffic at night. But there was a high school event letting out just then, and it took me fifteen minutes longer to get home than it would have had I gone through downtown.

~

I didn't think about Ben after his appearance on *Here We Are Now*. Our appearance. I listened to a couple later shows, in the weeks that followed. It came on as I sat reading computer drivel, and I half-listened for some reference that never came to what Ben had said when we were on, or something I'd said.

Three months later, Megan said something about Ben. We had been talking about her job, or she'd been talking about her job. I don't have that much to say about her job, except that she doesn't like it. She said, "You heard Ben got arrested."

I hadn't heard.

"It was in the newspaper," she said. "His photo, too."

That meant the police had used a Taser on Ben.

It's something they do in our town that I've never understood: when the cops use a Taser on someone, that person's mugshot appears in the newspaper. It's a form of public humiliation, I guess.

It's not the only form. When people are arrested, the police like to take them to their court appearances across a certain stretch of downtown. They park the van half a block away so that when the men and women climb out to walk the fifty feet to the courthouse, the whole town will see them in their orange jumpsuits.

They must have done that to Ben. He must have drooped his head so that his hair hung and blocked his eyes and his profile. It was what he had done when he got perturbed on *Here We Are Now*.

"What did he do?" I asked.

"What do you mean?"

"To get arrested."

"Oh. I'm not sure. I didn't read the article."

I exhaled. This was news, but it wasn't big news. People get arrested.

We talked a while about another friend and a problem she was having with her landlord. Then, when Megan was gone, I looked up the newspaper's website. There was Ben's photo.

He looked bad, like his face had been scraped against the sidewalk, or he had spent the night rubbing his face against sandpaper in his sleep.

The article said he'd resisted arrest. It didn't say what he was being arrested for when he resisted. It was a short article, about twenty words.

After a few seconds, I realized I wasn't breathing.

Ben hadn't resisted arrest. Ben wasn't the type to resist much of anything, let alone arrest.

I saw Julian across the room. He wasn't reading or talking to anyone. I don't think he has a computer. It's not for a good reason; he's just a trainwreck. I don't like him, but I knew he'd been arrested and would know what I wanted to know. He's kind of a Neanderthal, with a face like a disappointed caveman.

"Julian," I said.

"What?" he said.

"How do you visit someone in prison?"

"What?"

"When someone gets arrested," I said. "Where do you go if you want to see them at the prison?"

"They don't go to *prison* when they're arrested. That's for if you get sentenced. You mean *jail*."

"Whatever."

"It's like a fucking day camp. It's just bunk beds and guys jacking off."

"All right."

"It is."

"Well, where is it?"

"Route 10. West."

Fucking Julian. What he didn't tell me was that it's thirty miles outside of town. I should have just looked it up, but I'm at a point in my life that I'm tired of the internet, and if I can ask someone in person a question, I'll do it, even if it's Julian.

It turned out I couldn't just show up at the jail and see someone there. I had to make an appointment twenty-four hours in advance. So that was what I did.

But when I went back for the visit, the following day, calling in sick at the warehouse, Ben wasn't there anymore. He'd been released. They couldn't tell me where he had gone. "We stop keeping tabs on them," said the guard, in a voice that made me feel dumb, "once they leave here."

~

I lost track of him and his ordeal, whatever it was, for a while. I had my own problems, or, not problems, but the opposite of problems. I'd started seeing the woman I mentioned kissing before. I ran into her at a bar, and one thing led to another. It had nothing to do with Ben and the Vinyl Canal. It was great.

The only thing I don't like about her—her name's Ann—is that she does yoga to an audiobook, and the woman reading it sounds like Courtney Love reading Kurt Cobain's suicide note on MTV. She isn't crying quite like Ms. Love did, but she sounds like she's about to, like she is the Saddest Yoga Teacher in the World. Like she's practicing Sorrow Yoga. I can't be in the room when it's on, which isn't a problem, because Ann and I don't live together. We haven't moved that fast.

We've moved pretty fast.

Probably a month went slinking past without a word about Ben. Whenever I saw Megan, I expected to hear something, but I heard nothing. When I drove past the courtroom at the right hour, when the recently arrested were paraded in orange through the center of town, to be brought before the judge and the silent consternation of a mostly oblivious public, I looked to see if Ben was among them, to see if he'd been captured again. I didn't see him. I didn't expect to. I'm not sure what I was looking for.

~

I asked Megan, once, "Have you seen Ben?" She shook her head. "That's so strange," I said.

"What is?"

"The way he disappeared. I haven't seen him since he got arrested."

"I didn't know you saw him much before he got arrested."

"I didn't."

"So?"

I sighed and sipped my coffee. "It's just," I said, "what he said on the radio about police violence." Megan looked away, then back at me, confused. "This is a small town," I said. "What if they retaliated?"

"Because of something Ben said on the radio?"

"Yeah."

"I don't know, Jill," said Megan. "It seems like, if they retaliated against Ben for doing anything, it would be for the way he resisted arrest."

"I don't think he did that, though," I said.

Megan made a face. "You don't?"

I didn't think he had. But I didn't know.

81

I knew almost nothing about Ben. I wasn't friends with him on social media anymore. He wasn't on social media anymore.

~

Six months went by before I saw another sign of Ben.

It was like seeing the ghost of Ben, only Ben wasn't dead. I mean, he probably wasn't dead. I was at the bar Ann likes to go to, a music venue that's filthy and not my scene. It's Ann's scene. Ann is my scene.

It's the kind of place Julian goes, the kind of place where one wall is covered with flyers for shows that have happened or that will happen. I was on my way in, trailing behind Ann, who likes to go first, when I saw a flyer that was a black and white photo of Ben's face. Only it wasn't his face as I knew it; his left eye was swollen shut and his mouth looked like someone had sewn his lips together. It wasn't a good photo.

I thought I wasn't seeing it right. Of course his mouth isn't sewn shut, I thought. How could he eat? But there was something about the way his lips were pursed that made me think, My god, his lips are sewn shut.

The flyer was for a band called The Mud. Their show had been three weeks prior, on a night when I was out of town.

I asked some people there about The Mud, but no one had seen them. They hadn't even played. Mark spent ten minutes telling me how often bands will do that—plan a show and cancel it without taking down their flyers. It really seemed to bother him.

~

I went to a party where I thought I saw Ben. It was someone else.

Before he disappeared, I would have thought it was a good thing, that it wasn't Ben.

Megan was at the party. "What do you think happened to Ben, anyway?" I asked her.

"To who?"

"Ben."

"Ben Volpe?" Megan laughed. "I haven't thought about him in months."

Megan resumed asking me about Ann. I answered her questions, but my mind was somewhere else.

~

I realize now that my desire to know the fate of Ben has nothing to do with Ben. I still don't know what I would say to him if I saw him—probably nothing. I still don't want to be his friend, or a close acquaintance. But if he didn't just leave town because he wanted to, if he left because he had to, or if he's still around but not in a way I would recognize, then the possible explanations for that are not numerous.

If he left town, without warning or with it, it didn't mean something good had happened, that he'd had a revelation and saw how he was stagnating and had to rethink life. I know guys like Ben, and that kind of self-recognition isn't something they're subject to.

It would mean something bad had happened. There aren't many kinds of bad things that can happen in our town. Most of them involve the police.

I can't say I ever felt good about the police. I knew I would call them if I were stabbed, but when I saw one at

Prague's, getting takeout coffee, or a patrol car driving past, I didn't feel safer than I did when they weren't around.

Now that Ben was gone, I felt downright imperiled when they were near. If they knew who he was when he said what he said on the radio, and had made him pay for it, then maybe they knew who I was, too, and knew that I had sat beside him as he spoke.

I had gone to see him at the jail. Had that mattered?

Did they know my name?

I thought many times of going to ask after Ben at the police station. Surely they would know where he had been at some time. I thought better of it, every time, and didn't know if what I was thinking made any sense.

~

I told Ann about Ben.

I didn't need to tell her much. She had heard Ben on the radio. She had been the woman who called in, after all. She didn't know Ben, but she wasn't alarmed to hear that he'd gone.

"You don't know men," she said. "Not like you think you do. You think it's weird that a guy would just pick up and leave? No. Remember the town you're in. This place gets smaller the longer you're here. A lot of people—men especially—can't handle that."

Ann doesn't always know what she's talking about, but she's someone who always sounds like she knows what she's talking about. A lot of people can't tell the difference, which is her magic.

I can tell the difference. I knew she was just talking. Even if she knows men like she said she does, she didn't know Ben.

But it was what I needed to hear. What I wanted to hear. Ben seemed to have gone, but it didn't mean a thing, not necessarily.

~

Ann likes records. She has hundreds, most of them by bands I've never heard of. She is eager always to introduce me to them. I am not so eager to be introduced. But whatever.

When a new record store opened in town, Ann was overjoyed. She took me there the day it opened and got lost among the rows of vinyl by bands I'd never heard of. I'd heard of Sam Cooke, but they didn't have any Sam Cooke. I'd heard of Joni Mitchell.

I wandered until I found the dollar bin. I looked through it to find a lot of Barbra Streisand and Engelbert Humperdinck.

Beside the dollar bin was an as-is bin, where records cost only $0.25. In there I found some Jethro Tull and Tom Jones—not them performing together, but different records—then more Barbra, and then Tom Waits, The Beatles, James Brown and Blue Öyster Cult.

Wait a minute, I thought. These records didn't belong in the same bin as the garbage records someone had tossed out when their aunt died.

I looked at some of the records up-close, the ones that would be desirable had they not been tampered with. But they had been tampered with. They had grooves drawn in them, like the ones Ben had described on the radio, the careful etchings that helped them better suit their owner.

On some, Ben had etched his initials—BHV—into the outer edge. He must have been proud of what he had done.

Here it was, in the as-is section. The Vinyl Canal.

Ben had not described these records well. Or else, after his radio appearance, his devotion to the Vinyl Canal had only deepened, and the grooves he drew in the records grew more artful and elaborate. If the original scratches he left in *Agents of Fortune* were Doric, then the ones he made in *Electric LadyLand* were Corinthian; there were canals, and within the canals, where the needle wouldn't go, there were patterns I had never seen before. Layered onto the dull mass-market audio was visual artistry, amateur though it was. Ben had been like a monk writing on a palimpsest.

I had had no idea. But here it all was.

I looked at the covers of his records, at the magician with the deck of cards on *Agents of Fortune,* at Alice Cooper with a snake climbing down his throat, and at the Clash goofing off on the cover of *Combat Rock.* I thought of all the possibilities: Ben non-lethally subdued on Court Street, Ben slumped in his own vomit in the back of a police vehicle, Ben getting his ribs kicked in by a man in uniform.

Or: Ben packing his things, nonchalantly, probably while listening to a podcast, into whatever car he drove—a hatchback Civic, maybe—and peeling out of town because he didn't feel like being here anymore. He wanted to dive headfirst into Cleveland. Or Akron.

For one reason or another, he was gone. That was all it could mean, these records being here. They were his life's work, or the closest thing to it that there was.

I didn't buy the records. I didn't buy any of them.

From behind me, with a hand on my hip, Ann said she was ready to go. I rubbed my eyes and turned to leave with her.

Turkey of the Woods

On his blog, my friend Brian mentioned a place not far from town where I might find wild mushrooms if I looked, so as soon as I had a morning to spare, I got on my bike, said bye to Sherman, my Jack Russell Terrier, and rolled out. I brought my backpack and a glossy guide to the mushroom kingdom. Brian said he'd hit this spot a couple of weeks before, and I hoped I would find some morels he'd missed or that hadn't sprouted yet when he was there.

I was right. There were morels. I found them stuck to the sides of tree trunks and sprouting out of the wet dirt. I had gathered several handfuls of the edible fungus when I spotted a damp, old log where I thought there might be more. I peered underneath it, expecting some puffballs or a chanterelle. Instead, I found a brain.

It was stuck upside-down to the log, about half the size of a human head. At first, I didn't think it was a brain. I assumed it was one of the larger sort of mushrooms I'd seen in my guidebook, a Turkey of the Woods. I remembered its name because it seemed such an odd thing to call a mushroom, since actual turkeys live in the woods. In the book's glossy photos, it appears like a mass of overlapping tissues—not unlike a brain. So as soon as the rush wore off that comes with seeing what you're looking for but don't expect to find, I wrapped my hands around it and pulled. The brain was moist, like a mushroom—though also like a brain—and cold. It had not been in direct sunlight, or a head, for some time.

I had learned from the guidebook how to treat a mushroom in its habitat. I would have to pull it gently at first, then pull harder if it didn't break from its mount. The goal was to get out the whole fungus, and not just tear off the cap. This one was stubborn. It was the first mushroom that demanded I plant my foot on its residence and tug—even yank—until it came free. I nearly fell over backward when it did, and out spilled more blood than I had ever seen in one place.

It didn't spurt the way I've heard blood from an artery does, when connected to a beating heart. This brain had no heart, as far as I could tell. It came slopping out of the stem onto my sweatshirt and jeans, then drained to a trickle while I stood, astonished that a Turkey of the Woods would be filled with this cold, red fluid. I didn't recall reading in the guidebook that this sort of mushroom—or any sort of mushroom—would drain liquid on its forager, though I'd seen how a puffball grows to maturity then bursts with dusty spores when you squeeze it.

I slipped the brain into one of the roomier plastic bags I'd brought for the mushrooms, and into my backpack it went. I mounted my bike and pedaled home through the late morning. I didn't see any other body parts on the way.

When I arrived at my apartment, I checked my e-mail and washed my hands as Sherman sat sniffing my backpack where I left it on the floor by the door, his eyes fixed on the brain's latest vessel. He followed me through the house to the kitchen, where I carried our newest friend. He pointed his nose at the brain all the way. He's not tall enough to see over the counter, so he didn't see the brain when I pulled it out. He just sat and twitched his nose in the air, watching me. He would have barked, but he only barks when someone new comes over.

The bag was messy now—like a bag with a raw steak in it—blood pooling in the creases. The thing was still bleeding, which was another suggestion that what I'd found was not a mushroom. I didn't yet believe it was a brain, but I was struck now by how it resembled one. My house was warmer than the woods, so it had softened. When I pressed my fingers into it, it gave like it hadn't before; I could push half an inch into its surface, and it would spring back slowly like a drying sponge.

I don't know why I was so slow to realize that this was a brain. I guess I've always thought that plenty of things in the wild look and feel like organs, and so this was another one of those things.

I started to run some water in the sink to put the brain and mushrooms in, but then I thought better of that plan; I thought this specimen would be better off in something bigger. So I wrapped it in some paper towels and walked it to the bathroom. Some blood dripped out of the brain stem on the way, but Sherman went to work on that, licking it up as he came running behind me.

I ran the tub. As he sat looking up at the brain on the sink, Sherman frowned. I asked him, "What's up, buddy? Don't look like that. He won't bite."

I stood and watched him with my hands in my pockets as the bathtub ran and he kept staring at the brain, which I left on the edge where he could see it. When I tested the water, I realized I'd made it way too hot. I wasn't running a bath for a person—not a whole one, anyway—so I added some cold to the hot until it got lukewarm, and then it was time for the maiden voyage. I said, "Hey look out Sherman, he's gonna set sail," and he put his front legs up on the edge of the tub to see if our brain was seaworthy.

It floated. It hung at the surface of the water with its stem hanging down and a little to the side. It bobbed, and looked like it belonged there, almost like it was happy to be home, like I'd plucked a flower out of the ground and put it in a vase so it could live a little longer. The way the brain swayed gently back and forth, it seemed to have a mind of its own. As the dirt flaked off, I was more and more certain that this thing really was a brain.

But I wasn't sure if a real brain would float. I'd never done anything with a brain except think and move my body around, and dream, so I'd never tested one to see how it would fare in standing water. I didn't know any doctors I could call, and I didn't have health insurance, so I couldn't go see one. So instead I turned to my computer. I tried a Google search for "Do brains float?" It turned out, someone else had asked this question on a forum two years ago and had quickly gotten a response that told him yes, brains would float in water, since they basically float in liquid when they're in our heads.

That someone asked this question online made me wonder if I wasn't the only one to find a brain growing in the woods, so I googled "brain growing in woods." Results came back zero.

When I went to check on the brain, the water it was floating in had turned a little red, and I could see a trickle of deeper red coming out of the stem where I'd ripped it off. Sherman was sitting at my feet, looking up at me with that frown again, so I went to the freezer in the kitchen and removed the rubber band from around my bag of peas. I returned to the brain. I flipped it over in its natatorium, pinched the end of the stem together, and wound the band around it to stop the bleeding.

By then the water was cooling, so I drained some off and ran more hot to balance it out. I should have aimed for body temperature but didn't think of it at the time. I had to go to work, so I carried Sherman out of the bathroom and shut the door tight. As I climbed on my bike, I could hear Sherman whine under our front door behind me.

Work was a long haul. It was Friday, which meant a lot of families coming in for family dinner. I didn't get home until late. It was dark, the moon wasn't out, and someone stole my bike's headlight last month, so the ride felt longer than it was. The first thing I heard when I got home was Sherman, still whimpering at the door. I said, "Shit," because I'd forgotten all about the brain, and I'd been looking forward to a bath. I wasn't about to climb into the tub with it.

I took Sherman around the block. I had to drag him out, because he didn't want to give up his post. When I brought him back in and let him off his leash, he went running back over to the door, sniffing to see if our brain was still in there. He actually scratched at the door—something I had never seen him do.

If Sherman ever taught himself to open doors, it would have been then. But I was the only one there with hands, so I turned the knob and Sherman went charging in, his feet up on the edge of the tub as soon as he could get them there.

"Oh no, Sherman," I said when I joined him. "I don't think we did this right."

The brain was not in good shape. Thick layers of its outer tissue had turned to mush. It looked sick. It looked something like the half-eaten slices of toast that float in my dish pit on some mornings. They take on more water and expand and eventually break apart. The brain had been dissolving the whole time I was gone.

My friend Alvin told me once that when they autopsied Truman Capote, they found that all of the drinking had reduced the size of his brain by a big fraction—a fifth, I think—but he couldn't tell me what had happened to the rest of his brain. Where did that fifth of brain go? How does a brain shrink? Alvin didn't know. He said it must have swelled and peeled off—like what happened to the one in my apartment.

As I drained the tub, I asked Sherman if he remembered Alvin. He looked at me a second, then looked away.

Some of what had sloughed off the brain—brain sludge—fled with the water, down the drain. "That's gonna clog," I told Sherman, then thought, *No, that's gonna stink.* There was still a lot of brain left—just an outer layer had come loose, leaving most of it intact, looking a brighter pink than it had before, like raw skin under a blister, or the palms of my hands after work. I grabbed a towel—not one of my clean towels, but not one of the dirtiest ones—and wrapped the brain in it, setting it at the edge of the sink to let it dry.

I was in over my head, but I thought Brian might know what to do. He's more outdoorsy than I am, and handier, the kind of guy who knows what to do in situations. He's the one who got me into foraging, and he knows recipes for wild mushrooms—on his blog he has suggestions for what craft beers you should pair them with.

Back when I called Brian more often, I'd usually interrupt him doing something. He'd be out on his bike and have to pull over to answer, or he'd have to come in from his shed where he was working on a new set of shelves. "Hey Seth," he said when he realized it was me. "I was just out working on some shelves. What's going on?"

"Not a whole lot."

"It's been months. How's Sherman?"

"He's good. He's been eating."

"Yeah? Right now or in general?"

"Oh—in general. It's how I keep him alive."

"Yeah." He paused. "So what's up, Seth?"

"Well, I was hoping you could help me out with something, Brian. I went out to that spot this morning, looking for morels."

"What spot?"

"The one on your blog. Morel Compass."

"Oh, right, over by Grave Creek." He was quiet for a moment, probably picturing Grave Creek again in his mind. "I didn't know you foraged. Did you find anything?"

"Yeah, I did."

"Did you find morels?"

"Yeah, morels. It's the other thing I found I wanted to ask you about."

"Chanterelles?"

"No. Brian, have you ever found any body parts in the woods? Like any brains?"

Another pause. "What?"

"Well I found something out there I couldn't find in the guide. I thought it was a mushroom, but I think it's a brain. Can you hear me, Brian?"

"Have you been skipping meetings, Seth?"

"No, no. I've been at work. No, when I went out there, I found this thing I thought was one of those big ones you find sometimes, those guys you put up on your blog."

"A Turkey of the Woods."

"Yeah. But when I pulled it off the log it started bleeding. And it kept bleeding after I brought it home and put it in the tub. I had to go to work, but when I got back," I told Brian, "it was all waterlogged with pieces coming off. Have you ever heard of anything like that? I don't know if I can fix it myself."

He didn't talk for a few seconds, and when he did it sounded like he was having trouble getting the words out. "Seth," he asked, "is your brother still at his old number?"

"No, I don't think so, Brian," I said. "I'm fine. I've got Sherman here."

"I'm sure you do."

"I just thought maybe you could help me out. Are there any good web sites for this kind of thing?"

Whatever he said next, I didn't hear it. I dropped the phone, in fact, because I'd caught the unmistakable sound of Sherman getting into something. It's the only time he ever growls, when he's declared war on a roll of toilet paper, or I've left a box of cereal on the couch. Sometimes he can't help himself. He's a dog.

I must have left the towel hanging off the sink where Sherman could grab it with his teeth and pull it off with the brain that was wrapped up in it. When I found him, the towel was lying on the floor, and Sherman and the brain were on top of it. He was having his dinner early. He'd chomped our visitor down the middle, splitting him in half. Smaller bites lay broken up on the floor, like chunks of raw ground beef. There was blood. The whole bathroom looked like a crime scene.

For the first time I wondered what the police might think if they came in and saw all of this. What if I threw out what was left of the brain, and they went through my trash? What if someone came to unclog the brains in my drain and started asking questions?

So I let Sherman go at it. I hadn't fed him for the night yet anyway, and this way I wouldn't have to worry anymore about what to do with the rest of the brain. I didn't want to watch him eat, though, so I went into the other room and stood by my DVDs, waiting for him to finish. When he was done licking up all the last little pieces, he came out to join me.

He knew what was coming when he saw me standing there with my hands on my hips. I don't like scolding

Sherman, and he doesn't like getting scolded, but he knew he had broken the rules. Mister Man licked his chops and sat down. He looked at me. He looked away. He dropped his front half and put his face to the floor, his eyes fixed somewhere else in the room.

Then, with a whine, he looked right up into my eyes. For a few long seconds he kept it up, a frown about to form on his pup face.

There are two things I'll admit I'm no good at. One is teaching Sherman to not eat anything I don't put in his dish. The other is scolding him when he looks at me like he was. If he ever could have learned how to talk, it would have been then, so he could tell me how sorry he was for what he'd done. I shook my head and told him to come over here, as I bent down to take him up in my arms.

Lost Origins

Bree was trying on an orange skirt, and I was over by the register, waiting for her to come out of the dressing room.

They had a rack of VHS tapes by the register. Four for a dollar.

Before I knew it, I was browsing through those tapes. It wasn't because I wanted to buy one. It's how it is at a thrift shop. One second you're not browsing; the next second you're browsing, even if you're not passionate about what's there.

They had *Backdraft*. They had *The Addams Family*. They had a couple of tapes from Season One of *The Sopranos*. They had other things, too, like *Platoon*, which I had never seen. And there was a tape whose title appeared in plain white lettering, in small type, like someone had paid a fee to have it done at the local printer's shop or had used his own printer to do it. It was called *The Lost Origins of Reginald Ramis*.

The cover of the tape showed a grainy photo of "Famous" Reggie Ramis, who I had seen on David Letterman not one month prior. He was promoting something. I couldn't remember what. Definitely not this tape.

He looked young, on the cover of the tape. He had a moustache. Five minutes before then, even while *standing at that same checkout* (emphasis mine), I hadn't known Reggie

Ramis had lost origins. Now I had a chance to buy a tape that was all about them.

It's not that I was a fan of Reggie Ramis. I didn't even follow him on Twitter. I saw him a while ago in *Outbreakers* and wasn't impressed. I remembered seeing him on *Friend This!: Celebrity Edition*, the celebrity edition of the Facebook-based reality show. He seemed like just a regular celebrity, nothing special, somebody who's as likely as I am to have lost origins. And I definitely don't have lost origins; I'm from Columbus.

I got a basket. I threw in the tape. I added *The Addams Family* because tapes were four for a dollar. And so to make it an even dollar, I put *Platoon* in there, plus *The Crying Game*, because I thought I remembered Bree saying she liked it.

There was one problem: I didn't have a VCR.

When I found one in their electronics section for $2.99, I knew it could mean only one thing: problem solved.

With my movies and my new used VCR, I went to meet Bree at the checkout, where she'd been waiting for me. The tables had turned. She took one look at the contents of my basket and then looked at me. "I'm getting this," she said, holding up the skirt. "You're getting all that?"

"Yeah," I said.

"Why?"

"I don't have it yet."

She shrugged. We checked out, one after the other. If my total purchase had been more than four dollars, she or I might have questioned the wisdom of buying a VCR and tapes to go with it, when I have a computer that has Netflix on it, plus a bunch of Blu-Rays. But the VCR and tapes cost just four dollars. You don't question that.

The checkout lady said, as I was leaving, that she'd just remembered tapes were buy-four-get-one-free. I said,

"Whoa!" and went back and grabbed the first thing that looked good: *The Lord of the Rings*. Not the twenty-hour-long one, but the cartoon one my brother used to tell me about when we were growing up together, in Columbus.

Bree drove me home, where we said goodbye, but it wasn't time to do the VCR thing just yet. It was time to go work at Saddam's.

It's Saddam's Coffee Break—home of the Jet Fuel, which is coffee. There is nothing special about it. It just happens to be stronger than what you get at places like McDonald's, so they call it Jet Fuel.

Saddam's is not at the same location where it used to be. A decade and a half ago, the old place got firebombed because of the name, and because 9/11 had just happened. It's what I heard from Trina, another employee: after that incident, Saddam's moved farther away from campus. It was replaced with a college bar, The Heidelberg, which I've always thought was funny. Germans are the people everyone used to be mad at, not all that long ago. They were mad enough to throw lots of firebombs.

Work was busy. It's always busy. But I like it that way because the hours go faster when there's lots to do. When I got home eight hours later, feeling like I'd only worked two hours, it was nearly midnight. I wasn't tired because when I'm at work I drink the Jet Fuel, and I'm an insomniac.

Now was my chance to try the VCR. I watched *The Addams Family*.

One of the things I didn't know before I watched it is that Christopher Lloyd is a chameleon. The only things I'd seen him in were *Back to the Future*, *Back to the Future II*, *Back to the Future III*, and the Roger Rabbit movie. He's not really that different in those. But when he's Uncle Fester, you almost don't recognize him. He's that good.

When it ended, I was finally tired, so I went to bed. When I woke up late the next morning, I called Bree and told her Christopher Lloyd is a chameleon.

She had to go to work, she said. She had to go.

I took a shower. I didn't shave, since I'd shaved on Wednesday. I had the day off, but I didn't want to spend it inside because spring had sprung. I thought I'd go get some Jet Fuel, to start my day off right.

Trina was working. I knew she'd be working. It was half the reason I went there.

Trina's great. She wears big glasses, and she's probably the only girl who looks good in big glasses. On her arm is a tattoo of a hand grenade. When a lot of people get tattoos, they ask for hearts, or stars—a cool bug, maybe. Not Trina. She opted for munitions.

Saddam wasn't around, so she gave me the employee discount on Jet Fuel, which is what we call giving each other free stuff. She also gave me some biscotti before asking what I was doing later.

"Nothing," I said. "Bree's working late."

"That sucks," she said.

"Yeah," I said.

"Maybe we could do something," she said.

"Like what?"

"Big Bill's having people over."

"Oh yeah?"

"We should go."

"Okay."

"Cool."

"It *is* cool."

We said we'd meet at Saddam's at ten, then walk over to Big Bill's. He and Mike lived a few blocks from there.

Everyone was at the party: Gene, Phil, Candace. Gordy Meacham and Gordy Wumpus were there—and when they came in together, Gene said, "We got all the Gordys, yeah." Gene likes to call Gordy Meacham "Gourdy Pumpkin." Michael came late, and so did Molly, Holly, Sarah, and Kevin the Rat Charmer. They came in together, already drunk and laughing from the bars.

This was a different party in that Bree wasn't there, plus I kept holding hands with Trina. We didn't do it in front of everyone, only when she went behind the house to smoke a cigarette and I followed her there. We were just holding hands. We hadn't done it before. When she held my hand, a cigarette in her other hand, she stroked my palm with one finger. We probably would have done more, but people kept walking out to smoke with Trina and interrupted our progress.

Meanwhile, Bree was texting me, saying she wanted to break up.

Fine, I thought. I saw this coming. I could tell at the thrift store she wasn't into me anymore. It's better this way, I thought.

But I wasn't texting that back to her. I wasn't texting at all. I was talking to the people in front of me, living the analog life at the expense of the digital one.

I was trying not to think about Bree. I knew that if I did think about her, I'd get depressed.

Early in my relationship with Bree, I was at her apartment, in her room, and we'd just had sex for the first time when she went to her closet for a nightgown. Inside the closet I could see, from the bed, a huge box of Trojan Magnums.

This basically ruined the whole relationship before it started. I don't have a complex about my personal endowment—no more than the next guy. I'm not huge, but there's enough there, enough penis for whatever I need it for. It's average. There is nothing wrong with average.

Average can be great. But Bree kept evidence in her closet that there once was a monster cock in her room, and it had been there recently enough that she had to be prepared in case it came back. Half the time she was around, for the next month, it was all I could think about. Whose enormous thing was it? I'd wonder. Did she miss it when I was there? What about when I wasn't there?

It was fine with me if she wanted to break up, but I didn't want her to know it was fine with me. I maintained silence. She texted a couple more times. First it was, "You okay?" Then just, "?"

Trina walked me home an hour later. Then she came in, and we frenched on my couch.

Then we went to my room and had good sex.

She liked to be on top. She kept putting two of her fingers in my mouth. Then she put them all in except the thumb. When she orgasmed, I thought she was going to take my jaw off.

~

Trina was up already when I blinked awake the next morning. She had her hand on my chest, eyes closed, but she was awake. She said after a while that she was going to have a cigarette.

While she was out, I put on one of the tapes. I turned the sound off and thought it could just be on while we talked and ate Life cereal or whatever. The tape I put in was *The Lord of the Rings*. I wasn't paying attention, but I could tell it was a weird movie.

Trina and I talked a long time, mostly about Saddam's and people we both knew, which there are a lot of. We talked about the party. We would stop talking occasionally and watch the TV.

We had some Life cereal, and when we'd finished the Life, Trina went out for another cigarette. I switched tapes. I put in the one about Reggie Ramis, not really thinking about it.

Then I remembered Bree and how I'd still never texted her back. I wrote back, finally, "Thats cool," in reference to the breakup. Then, in another text, I wrote, "Ill see you soon." There is nothing more boring than typing an apostrophe.

When Trina came back in, she saw the TV and said, "What's this?"

"I don't really know," I said. I held up the box so she could see it.

She looked puzzled. She said, "'Reginald Ramis?' They mean Reggie Ramis, right? From *Tears of the Star*?"

"Yeah, and *MegaloManny*."

"That's right. And *Outbreakers*. That guy's a chameleon."

I did not agree with her there. But I wasn't about to start an argument. I was in love.

I turned up the volume, and we were silent as we watched *The Lost Origins of Reginald Ramis*.

What can I say? It was a triple-A mindfuck. About a third of it was made up of crude animation that I could hardly tell what the drawings were supposed to be. Another third was live footage of Reggie Ramis when he was young, and a lot of that was in slow motion. Another third of the tape was just gay porn with someone talking backwards over it. It kept going back and forth between those things, at one-minute intervals. I timed them, in my head.

The whole thing lasted twenty-seven minutes, according to the VCR.

We traded glances, Trina and I, throughout *Lost History*, but we saved our comments for the end. Trina was the first to speak. She said, "That was a weird movie."

"Yeah," I said as the tape rewound automatically, which I didn't realize it was going to do.

"What would you even call that? Is it a documentary?"

"No, I don't think so. It has an agenda."

"Documentaries can have agendas. Like *Triumph of the Will*."

"Was that a documentary?"

"Oh. I don't know."

We were silent for a moment. Trina said she needed a cigarette, so I followed her out to my front steps. She lit up and said, "Do you believe any of that stuff in there? About Reggie Ramis?"

"I don't know. About half of it seems possible."

"Yeah."

"The other half, I don't know."

"It's farfetched."

"It *is* farfetched." I paused. "But I'm going to be honest," I said. "I'm not really sure what it was trying to say."

"Yeah."

"And I wasn't sure what to do with all that gay porn."

"What were those voices *saying* when it was on?"

I shrugged and said, "Beats the hell out of me."

"And the animation was crap."

"You'd think they would have *narrated* some of that. What was it even about?"

"I think it was him getting divorced. He was in a courtroom."

"Really?"

"Yeah, there was that judge. In the robe?"

"Oh, that was a *judge*. I thought it was supposed to be a *Star Wars* guy."

"I didn't like the animation parts. I didn't like how they were silent."

"Me neither." The animated portions of the tape were probably the weirdest. They were the only parts that didn't have sound. The rest of it at least had backwards talking, or forwards talking, or the sound of sheer dread made into a sound. But during the cartoons, it was just nothing. All you could hear was me and Trina breathing and the sound of the tape whirring forward. "All that blood was no good," I said.

"That was blood?"

"Yeah, when the screen kept going red?"

"Bad news," Trina said. "Bad News Bears."

It really was bad news, Bad News Bears. And we would have talked more about it, but I asked Trina what time it was and realized I was a half-hour late for work. "Shit," I said. "Work!"

"You're working today?"

"Yeah!"

I ran inside, changed, brushed my teeth. I should have taken a shower, but there was no time. I had to get out of there. Trina said she could lock up for me. She said she'd see me at Rhody's.

When I got to work, forty-five minutes late and out of breath, Saddam greeted me like always. "Wa-halla-halla-halla!" he said. "Running a little late today!"

That was all he had to say about it. I put on my apron, and he handed me a mug of Jet Fuel. On his way to the back, he pointed to the cash register and said, "Register! Register, my man! Wa-halla-halla!"

Forty-five minutes late, and no one says a stern word. I wouldn't rather work anywhere else.

I don't know what "Wa-halla-halla-halla" even means. Saddam has always greeted me that way, and he greets everyone that way. I've thought about asking him why he says it, but I'd rather not seem ignorant of other cultures, so I just let it be. If it does mean something, at this point I'd almost rather not know because by now it's something I understand in my own way.

Phil came into Saddam's, later on. I asked him if he'd be at Rhody's. He said, "Yeah," like there was no question he would be there. Which there wasn't. I knew that. I'd only been making conversation.

And he was there, when I finally arrived at Rhody's around midnight. So was Trina. So was Trent, and so was Gordy W. All of them were drunk, but they acted pretty much the same, no matter what. When they drink, they laugh more. That's all.

For a while, I didn't even think about the *Lost Origins* tape, which I'd put in my jacket before leaving home because I thought I might show the tape to the people there. Rhody's has a TV and VCR in the corner by the ceiling. I had a High Life, then had another one, and then Gene came in. Someone outside had just kicked his bike for no reason. He was jacked up. "Who the hell would do that?" he said. "And for no reason!"

It was 1:30 in the morning when I pulled the tape out of my inside jacket pocket and stood on a chair to insert it into the VCR. I took out *Hellraiser III*, which had just ended.

I stood on the floor with my sixth High Life and watched the tape.

There was that old footage of Reggie Ramis again. And the animated trial stuff, or whatever it was supposed to be. And the gay porn.

The only audible reaction anyone had was to the porn. Someone said, "Christ," in a drawn-out way, when it first came on. But they weren't against it, not really. At least two of the guys in there were bisexual. We were not exactly at the hockey bar.

Aside from someone saying "Christ," I seemed to be the only one paying attention. The tape must not, I thought, be for group consumption. Which would make sense. It's not entertainment; it's an investigation of lost origins. It's meant to be taken in privately, on a one-person basis. Like a Björk CD.

When the tape ended and started rewinding, I realized I had been silent throughout this second viewing. Someone put the tape on the bar and put in *Re-Animator*, a favorite at Rhody's. I retrieved *Lost Origins* and returned it to my jacket.

I saw a few guys with their phones out, and I thought they might be looking up the *Lost Origins* tape on IMDB. Maybe they had caught its title and had gotten interested enough to google it. But I'd already tried that and come up with nothing. Which was perfect.

This movie was pre-IMDB. Pre-Google.

All of VHS is pre-Google. That's why I love it so much.

Rhody's was closing. So Gene, Trina, Gordy Wumpus, and I had to go to my apartment if we wanted to keep this up.

And we did. Trina, Gene, and I walked over there, while the others piled into Trent's car and said they'd meet us. They were going to get some beer on the way.

~

The rest of that night is a blur. I read somewhere that there's a scientific explanation for how, when you drink a lot and stay in one place, you remember it better than if you drink a lot and go elsewhere. I think that's why the first part of the night is so much clearer to me than the rest of it.

When we woke together the next afternoon, Trina asked what I remembered from the night before. I said, "We watched *Lost Origins*."

I had played it backwards, at my apartment. Gene had an app on his phone that would play up to ten seconds of video backwards, so I'd tried that on one of the gay porn parts, so I could see what the voice was saying.

I still couldn't understand the words, though. It sounded like someone was speaking German.

"He *is* speaking German," Dick said from the couch, where he'd been sitting and talking with Trina.

I'd forgotten that Dick had been there, at my place. He doesn't come around much.

When Jerry asked Dick how he knew it was German, he said, "I'm from Germany," which he is.

"Oh, man," I said. "Jerry was here?" Trina was nodding, like she'd remembered it first and was waiting for me to catch up.

Jerry was a great guy to have in some situations. He was like nobody else. You could rely on him to say exactly the right thing, but then sometimes he'd say the wrong thing, like when he told Holly to go fuck herself just minutes after Gene broke up with her. Then he sprayed beer on her jacket. He wasn't welcome at Big Bill's for a while after that.

Eventually, he apologized, and Gene forgave him for what he said to Holly. And most of the time he was mellow. You just didn't want to be around when he wasn't mellow.

I was remembering more, then.

I'd watched the tape a few more times. The third time, Gordy and I played it on fast forward while listening to Black Sabbath. Then we did that with *The Addams Family*, then with *Platoon*. It was a whole new way to watch movies. I wrote it out in permanent marker as an equation: Fast Forward + Black Sabbath = Good. I would later try it with *The Crying Game*.

Trina helped me remember more things from the party that slowly came back. She told me how much I drank. I was surprised to hear how much.

I wasn't completely surprised, though, because of how I felt physically. I was in bad shape. All night, I'd been sweating alcohol. I could feel it on my skin. It was like I'd been drinking in my sleep. Drinking formaldehyde.

It was time to get water.

When I walked into my living room, all the guys were still there, sleeping on the couch, sleeping on the floor. I didn't remember inviting them to do that, but I must have gone to bed with Trina before they left. Jerry wasn't there, and neither was Dick, but everyone else was dozing away. When I opened the door, they didn't move.

They started moving when the Jet Fuel started brewing. It never fails. I get it at an employee discount from Saddam's.

I took some aspirin and drank a half gallon of water. I looked into the living room, and Gene was sitting up, eyes half-open.

I remembered Dick telling us, the night before, what the voice was saying in German. He said it was someone counting down. The voice was distorted. It kept slowing down and going back to normal, like a warped record.

The numbers started somewhere in the five hundreds. Then it stopped while there was animation and old Reggie Ramis footage. Then, in the next porn section, the countdown was in the three hundreds, like it had still been counting through all the other stuff.

Only, the counting was slow, so it would have had to take longer than the intervening scenes lasted to get through all those numbers.

"There must be parts of the tape missing," I'd said. "They must have been edited."

Then I remembered other things. Things I didn't want to remember.

I remembered watching the tape a fourth time with Gordy while Gene and Dick went into my room with Trina and shut the door. I remembered thinking they were getting high. But then, it didn't smell like weed in my room when I went to bed with Trina, after they'd gone.

Trina was smoking a cigarette by the window, holding it outside and blowing smoke out there where I returned with Jet Fuels for us both. It was raining. Bad hangover weather. Bad memory weather.

Trina knew something was wrong. "What is it?" she said.

I couldn't even speak. I shut the door and locked it. I sat on the bed and started crying.

"What's wrong?" asked Trina. "What's going on?"

I asked Trina what she did in my room with "those two guys" the night before.

She took me in her arms and stroked my hair. She didn't say anything. And I was kind of glad about that. I didn't really want to know what had gone on in there between the three of them.

I'm at a point in my life where a lot of things that used to matter don't matter as much as they used to. Like, I don't see that much of a difference anymore between a hand job, a blow job, and actual sex; to me, they're all examples of intimacy, and one of those things isn't any worse than the next.

I knew that at least one of the things that isn't worse than the others had happened in my room the night before then. It had happened between three people, and I wasn't any of those people.

It didn't hurt all that badly. If that's how people want to be in a room when I'm not there, I thought, then so be it.

110

I've still got legs and hands. I have a job. I have *The Crying Game* on VHS.

The bottom line was, it was the beginning of the end of me and Trina.

And, of course, I learned much later what really happened in there between her and our friends. They were in my room a long time, it turned out. I'd passed out on the couch and not remembered. By the time I woke up and went back into the room, my friends had left, leaving Trina in bed, serene and ready for me to join her. There were no blow jobs or hand jobs while I was gone, just straight-up sex, all three of them on my bed.

I don't know whose mouth Trina put her hand in. Probably not both mouths. That wouldn't be a very sexy thing for her to do. It might even mean that she had some kind of problem.

I knew as much as I knew because Trina told Jerry all about that night, six months later, when they started going out. Then, one night at Rhody's, after they broke up, Jerry told me what Trina had said. She hadn't mentioned *Lost Origins*. Instead, she'd said her first three-way took place that night. Or, at least, her first three-way with two guys.

Jerry said Trina was "a triple-A whore," then threw his empty High Life bottle at the stage, where a band was playing. It was the kind of thing that got him banned from Rhody's a few times a year.

And while I said a minute ago that I have reached a level of maturity in my life, with sex, where I'm nonjudgmental—and while I did not appreciate the way Jerry was slut-shaming Trina—it doesn't change how much what Jerry said hurts when you hear it. There's no reason why it hurts—it just does.

There was more. Jerry said he was the one who taped over *The Lost Origins of Reginald Ramis*. He said he had tried

111

to watch it again at my place after everybody else fell asleep and I was in my room with Trina in my arms—"like she hadn't just taken a double-dog pounding and loved it," he said with no regard for Trina's feelings. But instead of pressing Play, he pressed Record. That was why, when I tried to watch the tape again, it was just twenty-seven minutes from the middle of the movie *Dragonheart*, which I don't even like, but which was on Showtime when Jerry pressed Record.

I never confronted Trina about how she handled the situation that night at my apartment. By the time I found out what really happened, a lot of time had passed, and I was with Bree again. That night with Trina was water under the bridge, and I didn't even like the bridge anymore.

But one of the other things I remember from that night was that before Dick penetrated Trina I told him a theory of the Reggie Ramis tape. I said there must be other tapes like this one in the world. "Who knows where," I said. I said they must have different contents, all the different tapes, but what they had in common was the countdown. "The numbers they don't say on this tape must be on the other tapes. Maybe the numbers are in German on them, but maybe not. Maybe they're in Japanese."

I talked a while longer about what it would be like to find all the tapes and play the counting parts in order. What would happen then?

I have tried tweeting at Reggie Ramis about his lost origins. He never tweets back.

I think about this stuff all the time.

On Brian's Dreams of Submarines

I knew before Michael opened his mouth that he wanted something from me. He has this way of pursing his lips and looking grim that indicates when he is about to assign me a task that is not in my job description. He said hello and asked, standing as close to Bridget as he does when addressing either one of us, if I would go and make sure that a particular desk on the far end of the office was clean and its drawers were empty.

He was referring to the desk where Brian used to work. Soon, Michael said, someone new would finally replace him. I was halfway out of earshot when he thanked me for "taking care of this" for him.

On the whole, the desk looked fine, which reinforced my suspicion that Michael only gave me this thing to do so that he would have an excuse to engage Bridget in a conversation once I'd left them alone. There were some paper clips in Brian's top-left drawer. I let them be.

In the opposite drawer was something very different. It was a three-ring binder, on its surface just like the dozens of others I see in this office every day. When I looked into this one, however, I did not find the industry analyses and investment predictions that are our company's products.

It was a diary. It was Brian's diary—left behind, I suspected, when he quit his job. It was not handwritten. It was typed, on loose-leaf paper.

It was organized, too. Entries were arranged chronologically, as in most diaries, but Brian had added an index and table of contents. As I examined it further, in the few minutes I spent at Brian's desk, I learned that this was no mere diary but a dream diary.

I didn't leave it there with the paper clips. I brought it with me to my end of the office.

By the time I returned to my desk, Michael was gone, and Bridget was on the phone. I slid the diary in between some other binders that looked just like it, on the shelf above my computer. I didn't take it down again until that afternoon, when, as I ate lunch at my desk, I began reading.

My timing was regrettable, for as I dug into the leftover pasta I'd brought to work, the first entry in Brian's dream index to catch my eye was "Vomit, person eating." There were four listings. Brian, it seems, dreamt repeatedly that he was at a restaurant, sitting across from a man, a stranger who ordered the same thing every night: soup served in a bowl made of bread. Partway into the meal, the man would gag, and retch, as soup began pouring from his mouth back into the bowl. Out of some "effort to be polite," Brian called it, the man would try to keep eating the soup, but would only vomit more, as Brian—also polite—sat with his own food and didn't say anything. That was the whole dream.

Another index entry read, "Mother, metamorphosed." Apparently, Brian dreamt often of his mother. That was nothing unusual in itself, but in many of those dreams she was transformed into something nonhuman. Once, she was a Sherman tank with whom he pleaded for his life, but because she was a tank, she could respond only by rolling forward on her treads, so slowly that Brian could hardly tell she was moving. In another dream she was a chess board on which he played game after game against himself, alone.

"Lost to myself every time, somehow," he adds, then: "Woke up exhausted."

Not all of Brian's dreams were exhausting or disgusting, however. He dreamt often that he could fly, something he seems to have enjoyed. In one dream he chose not to fly, even though he was perfectly capable of doing it. In another dream, a lot of Japanese women ran in terror from his best friend, who wandered the streets of their hometown with an axe driven into his head. "Drove to work happy," he concluded.

Bridget didn't ask what I was reading. Because the diary was bound as it was, it looked just like the thousand other three-ring binders we keep in our office. She must have thought I was working through lunch.

It didn't occur to me until lunch was over that this must have been exactly what Brian had in mind when he kept his dream diary in a binder rather than a notebook. He must have typed and bound his journal in order to disguise it as something filled with work-related things. Because it looked so unsuspecting, Brian could get away with writing in it at work. Michael would walk by and see the dream journal but be clueless as to what it really was.

The journal's mimicry is convincing, and thorough. Our industry reports have graphs in them, and so Brian's dream report has graphs in it, too.

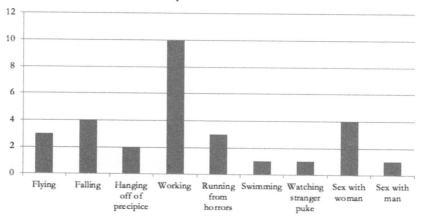

Dreams had by theme - November 2010

Figure 1

Brian had a lot of dreams. The journal covers only his dreams from October to August of last year, but it is nearly three-hundred pages long. He had more dreams in a span of ten months than I have had in as many years. It is no wonder he needed an index.

~

Brian didn't work here long. He lasted about ten months. It says as much as I need to know about how essential his job was that it took half a year for someone to replace him. He never made an effort to get to know the rest of us in this office, so I didn't know him well. Most of what I did know about him I gathered from walking past his desk, where he ate all his lunches. I remember his shirts were too big for his body. I remember he didn't eat very much.

It occurred to me, the day I found the dream journal, that I should probably try to return it to Brian. I thought it might

116

be his only copy, and he might want to have it back. I asked Bridget if she had Brian's address, or e-mail address. She had neither. She said she'd forgotten all about him until Michael mentioned his empty desk that morning. Then she asked why I was asking. I didn't say.

If Michael had ordered Bridget to clear the drawers of Brian's old desk, she would have glanced at this diary once and promptly sent it through the shredder she keeps beside her. I couldn't say why I didn't do that myself. I didn't have to say why. I kept its discovery a secret.

That was not something I had planned to do. In fact, the first thing I thought when I found Brian's journal was that I was going to have to take it home and share it with my husband, whose name is also Brian. I was halfway through drafting a midday e-mail to him, to tell him about the diary, when I hesitated.

I wondered if Brian would be as willing as I was to pore over the private writing of another Brian. He might try to convince me to throw the journal away or put more energy into tracking down its author. He might say that reading it was morally problematic, or at least rude. So for the time being I kept it to myself, and began reading it cover to cover, like a book, in lunch hours that followed.

I nearly gave up on it after the first sixty pages, which covered the first two months Brian worked in the office. This first act contained mostly dreams bizarre but benign— more scenes of his mother transformed into objects; more lunches with the man who devours his own vomit; sex dreams; work dreams; some nightmares of hanging off ledges, sometimes falling; and dull dreams in which he is forced to return to high school and repeat the tenth grade.

In December, though—on page eighty—he had his first dream in which he murdered another person. "At a New Year's party," he wrote. "At work. I sneak into a dark room with a co-worker. When her head is turned, I pull her hair and smash her face against the Xerox machine. Dead in seconds."

I laughed when I read this, it seemed so unsuited to the Brian I never knew but glanced at from time to time, his headphones over his ears as he sat as his desk doing nonessential work and munching salads. He didn't look like he could harm anyone. He was tall but he was skinny—lanky, even—which was something his oversized shirts only made more apparent. He must have been in his early twenties, but he looked like a teenager.

He wrote nothing in the way of explanation for the Xerox murder dream. He offered no analysis. There are no clues as to whether he fantasized about the crime prior to the dream, if he was pleased to have had it, or who it was he dreamt of killing—one of his real co-workers or some fictional stand-in. There is a surprising lack of dream analysis in Brian's dream diary.

What I didn't realize as I read that entry, and what Brian didn't know when he wrote it, was that this office party dream was only the beginning. Brian continued to dream often of harmless things, like public schools he had gone to and movies he'd seen. He had the obligatory dreams in which he made mistakes at work and couldn't fix them. But the dreams in which he murdered people grew more frequent.

I, who have never had one such violent dream in my life, found the number of his victims staggering. As if to facilitate my getting across how staggering the numbers are, he made a bar graph, to document the methods of his murders.

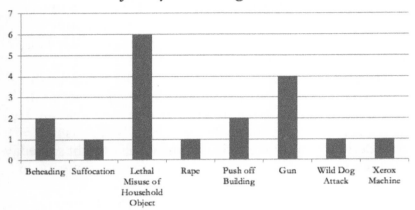

January 2011 Killing Methods

Figure 2

If I had turned to this page first, when I found the diary, before I knew it was a dream diary, I would have been a great deal more alarmed than I was. I would have had to call the police or bring the journal to Michael's attention and hope he called the police. As it was, though, all I did was question Brian's capacity to make bar graphs.

Brian's goal in Figure 2 was to track the ways in which he killed people in his dreams. But the fourth category— Rape—is not murder. Why Brian thought it belonged on the graph is beyond me. It occurred to me at first that Brian may, in fact, have dreamt that he raped someone to death, or that he had a dream of tremendous length in which he committed rape only to watch his victim for days afterward as she lost the will to live as a result of his having violated her. But from reading the entry in which he describes this dream, it would seem instead that Brian simply didn't obey the criteria of his bar graph, and included this crime in it, which, for all its awfulness, is not murder.

Brian describes his rape dream in the same tone with which he describes most of his dreams. He keeps a nearly clinical distance from the dream's contents, rendering them almost as if the dream belonged to someone else. He fails, as usual, to complete most of his sentences.

"Trapped in an alley," he begins. "Under attack by three thugs—two men one woman. I knock the men out, hard."

The next part I will paraphrase: he rapes the woman. He then adds, in a complete sentence at entry's end, as if considering for a moment that someone else might someday read his journal, "I have never wanted to rape someone in waking life, ever."

It was not lost on me that if Brian dreamt of raping a woman, it might have been one of the women in this office. It might have been me. But he doesn't mention his victim's name. He never names his victims, unless he dreams of killing someone famous. It was when he drank, which wasn't often, that he dreamt of killing celebrities. These included Phoebe Cates.

That "Rape" is on the bar graph of dream-killings is not its only problem. The category "Lethal Misuse of Household Object" is misleading. If you look into the entries, he's really misrepresenting a more diverse range of killings. Mostly he is stabbing people with kitchen knives and bludgeoning them with bookends, which is really what lethal misuse of household objects would have to be, unless you drowned a man in a fish tank, which he never mentions doing in his dreams.

The one category should be two categories. With this apparent inattention to detail, it is no wonder he didn't last longer at his job than he did.

~

I have had to ask myself, because I don't have Brian here to ask, why it is that he put so much effort into organizing his dream journal. For it is an organized journal, and Brian was a diligent—even pedantic—diarist. He went so far as to determine the gender distribution of his dream populations.

Dream Populations by Gender,
March 2010

Women
Men

Figure 3

The diary's graphs and charts are, on the one hand, merely part of the document's work disguise. It could be that they are frivolous and entirely without meaning.

That is, I think, how they got started. I don't think Brian meant anything by them at first. But it's clear that he got more invested in them than he expected to. With the appearance of Figure 3 in the diary, he describes the painstaking effort it took him to come up with its numbers. After work, sometimes, he would nap with a notebook beside him, so that he could wake up and tally his dream's citizenry before they faded from view. He dreamt, one afternoon, that he was caught in the middle of a large crowd of oblivious people as he strangled a long-haired teenager who turned out to be his younger self. When he woke, he tried to estimate how many members of the crowd had been women, how many men.

He didn't respond to his strange and violent dreams by starting therapy. He didn't read Freud. I can't say I blame him for that, as I find even the most compelling dreams ultimately meaningless. Still, I can't explain why Brian did things like document the race distribution of the people he saw in his sleep.

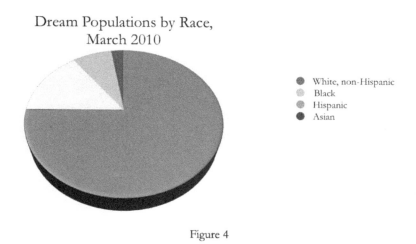

Figure 4

There were times when I wondered if this journal was a ruse, something written up as a practical joke by Michael and placed in Brian's desk where he knew I would find it when asked to look there. That, I thought, would explain the absurd misdirection of Brian's dream analysis, in which he makes no effort that I recognize to figure his dreams out and instead treats the people in them like strangers in a government census.

Dream Populations by Age,
March 2010

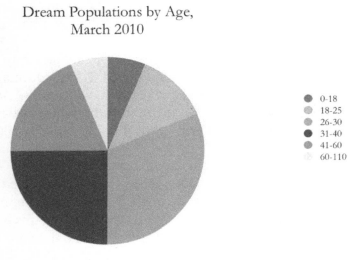

Figure 5

But I couldn't accept that. Somehow I knew this was a genuine document. I didn't know why Brian's "Race" pie chart was 3D, when the others were two-dimensional, but I felt certain it was not something Michael would think of.

~

I rarely have dreams that are interesting enough to write down, but once Brian's dream journal entered my life their plots thickened. They weren't like Brian's dreams. No one was transformed into an engine of war. I didn't kill and eat my friends.

I dreamt, one night, that I had a laughing baby. I dreamt that I slept in a trashcan. I dreamt that heaven was my high school cafeteria—a big disappointment. I dreamt that a British man from a restaurant show I watch gave me cooking advice, but it was all bad advice I couldn't follow if I wanted to. "The first ingredient you put in any dish," he implored, "should be tears of joy."

I told some of these dreams to Brian—husband Brian—as we ate breakfast, but he wasn't interested. It takes him an hour every morning to be ready to engage with the world, and he'd only been awake for thirty minutes when I relayed my dreams to him, so that was part of it, but I also think he just didn't care.

I developed a theory, that dreams are interesting to people other than their dreamer only when they've been written down and processed through the act of writing into something more concrete. If I wrote down my dreams and left them in a folder in the apartment, Brian might find them when I was dead or at a conference, and he might be as engrossed in my dreams as I was in those had by work-Brian. I realized at the time that this was not a credible theory so much as it was something to think about at breakfast, as I sat across the table from my silent husband, who was lost in thoughts of his own.

~

Later that morning, I asked Bridget if she dreamt often. She said "No," and added that when she does, she usually dreams of being at work, doing her job, so the less she dreams the better.

Her comment—that when she dreams the only thing that stands out is the setting—made me realize that one thing Brian did not keep track of, for the first three-quarters of his diary, were the locations his dreams were set in. When he cut off a man's hands and watched him crawl around and bleed to death on the night of March 12th, he could have been anywhere. He neglected to mention where any of his dreams took place. The only exceptions were when he dreamt of being at work—which was rare—and when he dreamt of burying someone alive. Again, I am most curious to know who his victims are—and he almost never says— but it is in these live burial dreams that he offers locations. He is in his backyard, or in a rainforest.

Dream locations became much more important to Brian on the night of May 5th. That was the first night he dreamt of being on a submarine. "I am on a submarine," he wrote. "I am in a cot. Surrounded by people. Sub is crowded. I leave the cot. I make my way aft." Brian makes his way "aft." There he sabotages the submarine, killing everyone onboard as the sub tilts dramatically in the direction of the hole he has made in the ship, through which pour thousands of gallons of seawater. As he slowly drifts back to waking—coolly, calmly—the people who have watched him do this thing panic and drown.

From that night on, he dreamt of waking up on the submarine and sabotaging it every night until the end of the diary, on August 5th, the day he quit and disappeared from the lives of me, Michael, Bridget, and the others who took so little notice of him when he was here.

It is the only dream that recurs, night after night, for any period of time, and it does so for months. There are just a few nightly variables, such as his method of sabotage. Sometimes he uses a bomb, sometimes a jackhammer, other times he simply punches his fist through the hull in a way that no one ever could.

One result of this turn his dreams took was a dramatic increase in the number of his victims, made starkly apparent in Figure 6, which appears on diary page 203.

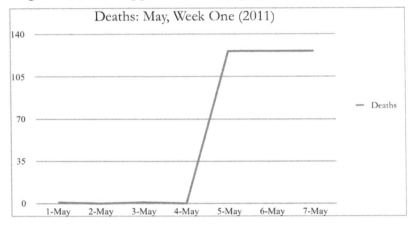

Figure 6

He had never even been on a boat, he wrote. It made no sense to him that he should have such dreams as these. He went looking through his daily life for reasons why the dreams were recurring, why he found himself night after night onboard the same vessel. He used his waking life as a place for sorting out his sleeping life. He stayed up late one night watching *The Hunt for Red October* on television. At first this struck me as counterproductive, but he wasn't trying to stop the dreams, only figure them out. Then I remembered that I'd watched the same film, the very same night on the same channel, miles away in my apartment, with my Brian asleep in the other room.

~

The number of people Brian killed on the submarines was an exact and consistent number: 125. It is not a figure he made up. It is the number of crewmen who were aboard the K-19—the Widowmaker—the first-ever submarine to be equipped with nuclear warheads. Built by the Russians, it earned its name because its construction was so hazardous that people were likely to be killed just putting it together. In 1961, the Widowmaker had a crisis, a near meltdown of its nuclear reactor. You don't have to be Tom Clancy to know this; it's all online.

Brian, who didn't have Wi-Fi access at home, had an illustrated history of twentieth century warships in his apartment, given to him by his father before he died. One night before bed, he went looking through this book for the submarine he had been dreaming of. He found it in the Widowmaker. "Eight pages on Widowmaker in this book," he wrote. "Big photos of interior. I recognize its corridors from my dream. Engine room identical." There, the entry ends.

Brian convinced himself that the sub of his dreams was the K-19. It seems likely that this was wishful thinking on his part. I doubt he really conjured up in his head at night the historically accurate interior of a real submarine.

All the same, he seemed to get something out of this link between his dream life and his waking life. I can't say what it was. He offers nothing in the way of explanation for what it told him about the dreams or why he had them.

It is clear enough, though, that something about the sheer numbers of the men he killed on the sub made Brian uneasy. Many pints of blood had poured from his victims in prior dreams, without making him flinch, but this elevated body count troubled him. It made him want answers for what was happening in his brain when he wasn't awake to control it. It doesn't look as if he ever found the answers.

I think this problem with the numbered dead was a red herring. To me, it seems self-evident why the submarine dreams bothered Brian so much. Clearly he was invested in dreaming, enough that he maintained his journal of them with great dedication. To have all of his dreams become nearly identical to one another must have been a nightly disappointment for him.

This answer, which seems so clear to me, did not occur to him. Instead he made another gender pie chart, reflecting his new dream populations.

Gender, June 2010

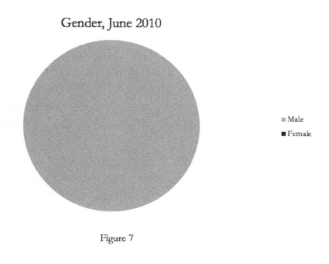

Figure 7

~

Jim, Brian's replacement, joined our staff a week after I cleaned out his desk to make way for him. The first thing I learned about him was that he wore cologne, in this place where men usually smell like nothing. The second thing I noticed was that he thought he was handsome. There is a way in which certain self-assured straight men from the Midwest smile at women. It is a smile I suspect is involuntary. They get so excited to know you're looking at them, and they're so confident they know exactly what you're seeing, that they can't help themselves. If you fail to smile back, they take it as a personal affront, even if most of them don't say so. Bridget smiles back, and so Jim frequently writes her e-mails and arrives to say hello while I'm off making copies. He sits in my chair, so that when I return, I have to ask him if I may have my chair back please.

I knew more about Jim by the end of his first day than I knew about Brian the whole time he worked here. In Jim's long first conversation with Bridget, he said he was a point guard in college, that he moved here from Indiana, and that he liked being nearer to the ocean.

That night, I mentioned to my Brian that every time he'd cooked dinner in the last two weeks, he had made the very same thing, a recipe involving pasta and chicken he learned from his mother. He did not take it well, this mention of what was a plain, recent reality in our kitchen, which I intended as a sort of constructive criticism. No one likes to eat the same thing so often, I said.

I ate cereal for dinner. Then I went to sleep and dreamt that I was still at work, listening to Jim tell Bridget about his life before he lived so close to the ocean.

~

What bothers me most about Brian's dream diary—much more than the nature of so many of Brian's dreams—is that I cannot determine whether he included himself in his submarine death tolls. The number of casualties in all his recurring nightmares holds steady at 125.

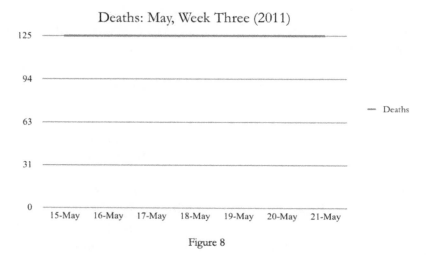

Figure 8

At first, I assumed that in these dreams Brian was a member of the crew, so that in his nightly count of 125 dead he was the 125th. Later, I didn't think so. He noted on the morning of July 5th that in his dream the night before he passed a mirror and saw he wasn't dressed like the others onboard.

He was, I gathered from this, an imposter. He wasn't one of the 125, he was number 126, the one who never shows up on any of the graphs.

This is despite the plain reality that if Brian sank a submarine when he was onboard it, he was going to die as well. He doesn't describe the experience of drowning—he either leaves that off, or he always woke up before the water reached his lungs—but surely he knew that he would drown at the conclusions of the dreams.

Still he does not appear in the graphs. He excluded himself from them. He never considered that he would have suffered as much as his victims did.

Brian did lose sleep, though—something that never happened as a result of his earlier, bloodier nightmares. I don't know if something else was going on in his life to make this happen. I doubt it. For several nights in August, when he'd been dreaming of the subs for three months, he didn't sleep at all.

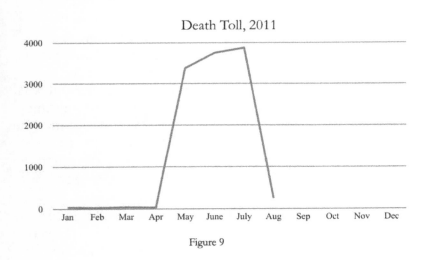

Figure 9

Brian made his last line graph—Figure 9—on the last day he worked here. For me and Bridget and Michael and the others, it was just another day with quiet Brian in the building, but the final graph makes it clear that for him it was the end of something. The line drops as sharply and abruptly as he dropped out of our peripheral vision.

Michael said Brian never gave him notice, never wrote or called to explain why he wouldn't be coming in again. He must have slipped his journal into the desk drawer and forgotten it there as he fled our office for the last time. Then he was gone.

~

On the night of February 11th—the day I finished reading Brian's dream journal—I finally shared my discovery with the other Brian, my husband. I have not mentioned it outright, but I haven't tried to keep it a secret, that in months prior he and I had been growing apart. It wasn't just the breakfasts he spent half-asleep. It wasn't just my sleepless nights. It wasn't just the pasta with chicken. It was that we spent so much of so many of our days commuting in opposite directions—he into the city, I farther out into the suburbs—and working in buildings far apart from one another. When I finished the journal, when I'd devoured it all in secret, I decided that keeping it from him hadn't helped anything.

It was late at night, in our kitchen, that I brought the dream journal to Brian's attention. He was eating leftovers and reading a book. I said, "Will you look at something with me? I want you to see this."

He sighed and turned to me, probably expecting me to show him something from work—which I was, though not in the way he expected. And because of the journal's outward appearance, it took him the same moment it had taken me, to realize this thing bore no relation to my work.

At first, he seemed as put off as I had been by the contents of some of Brian's dreams, but like me, he was more intrigued by them than alarmed. After all, he said, "They were only dreams. It's not like the guy really killed anybody."

Brian said he'd had plenty of dreams as bad as Brian's, that in high school he had a series of them in which he hacked his father apart with an axe.

I had not known this about my husband.

Nor was he surprised that Brian had dreamt of being on the same submarine every night for so long. He said that whenever he is stressed out long-term, he dreams he is an astronaut, trapped in a tiny spaceship he can't bring back to earth. That wasn't too different from dreaming of a submarine, he said.

When I told Brian my theory as to why Brian the diarist never shows up on the casualty reports, he refused to accept my explanation. He insisted that Brian was indeed one of the 125 dead. "But," I pointed out to him, "he says right here he wasn't dressed like the rest of the crew. He wasn't one of them."

Brian asked, "Well, what if he was an officer? What if he was the captain? Don't they dress differently from the other men on a submarine?"

I knew the answer to this, as I'd recently watched *The Hunt for Red October*. "Yes," I admitted to Brian. He was right about that.

We were, as it happens, talking more about the dream diary than we had talked about anything on any evening in recent memory.

We stayed up late, both of us, with the diary. Then we went to bed together, at the same time, something that hadn't been happening lately. It was an experience I'll describe using a technique adapted from Brian's journal.

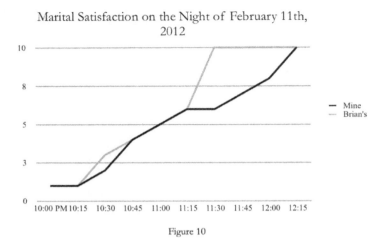

Marital Satisfaction on the Night of February 11th, 2012

— Mine
--- Brian's

Figure 10

When both of us were equally satisfied, as it were, we dozed off. We slept nearer to one another than we had in months.

I had a dream that night, that I was walking alone on a beach. It was night. Lying on the shore were hundreds of silent babies. I ignored them.

I sat down in the warm sand and watched the stars fall out of the sky, one by one, until I woke up and found myself in Brian's arms.

Cadiz, Missouri

I never had much use for Cadiz. I don't mean the port
city in southwestern Spain, though I've never had any use
for that Cadiz, either. The one I have in mind is at the heart
of America, and despite the way it's spelled the residents
pronounce its name like "callous," its z become an s that
hangs limp from their tongues. If you say it the Spanish
way, they correct you.

Whereas the original Cadiz was founded in the ninth
century BC by some Phoenicians who settled in the path of
a prominent trade route, I cannot imagine why America's
Cadiz was built where it was. It was not built on the river,
or the interstate. There were no trade routes running
through it. You couldn't get a decent sandwich there, at
least not on the Saturday I spent exploring it with Charlie,
soon after we moved nearby. There was never a reason to
go back after the first trip. They had a nice courthouse—I'll
give them that—but if you've seen one granite courthouse,
you've seen them all.

Our Cadiz did not share the longevity of its Spanish
namesake. It stood barely a century and a half. The first
Cadiz has survived invasions, pirate attacks, and the Franco
regime, but its American counterpart was wiped out in
minutes by a rogue weather pattern. The town hardly
deserved its name.

I would say that I regret not seeing more of Cadiz when I
had the chance, but there was nothing to see there except

doomed houses. They weren't worth looking at until we found out they were doomed, and by then it was too late.

~

When a tornado comes to take away your house, your pets, and your neighbors, it comes as a surprise, but if you live in Missouri, you expect one every time the weather looks like it might turn against you, which it does in summer months several times a week. I watch always for the slightest misbehavior of a thunderstorm; I know all the cues for catastrophic weather.

My first thought, every time I hear about a new tornado, is that if one comes to my house I will have to go huddle in my basement. Something I learned when I moved to Missouri: if your basement is old and you don't have a fortune to spend on restorations, a rainy day will flood it waist-high with grime and disease. Ours is a space we never use, a part of our house that serves no purpose, except as a habitat for strange insects.

For if the water in our basement were not a problem, still there would be cave crickets. They are massive and look like spiders; they're often called cricket spiders. With legs thick and black, they don't move until you come close, and when you do, they leap across the room. It's terrifying.

So on the morning in July when the rain got suddenly harder than it had been since I woke up, the sky turned slightly green, the warning siren went off, and at the same unlikely time I saw the clouds out my window surge east as if their cloud-lives depended on it, my first thought was not of my impending death, but of the creatures in my basement. I am embarrassed by this, but it is true; in my mind, the threat of physical contact with big insects outweighed the fact of real mortal danger. I froze, hoping I could stay where I was and simply watch the sky restore its recent shade of gray, but for a long minute it only got more green, and soon the green verged on black. The air looked sick, like an ailing cumulonimbus had ruptured and drained bile into the lower atmosphere. I didn't see or hear a cyclone, but if I had it would have seemed an afterthought, a side effect of the Missouri sky, the sight of which was like the sight of a solar eclipse to those who don't know what it is.

If this had been forty or sixty years ago, I would have heard cellar doors slamming over the siren as mothers shuttled their children to safety, but everyone here works during the day, and I seem to be the only one who does it at home.

As it happens, the tornado spared me and the furniture, and my legs were spared getting soaked with cellar water. Within a minute the green dissolved, and the storm behaved again like a typical storm.

When I looked online, I heard the news that our neighboring village of Cadiz had just been reduced to eight square miles of shredded houses and overturned cars. The whole town was destroyed in minutes—minutes I had spent fearing the same ruin they suffered, even as they suffered it. Having seen nothing of interest in Cadiz when I was there in person, now—through my TV and computer screen—I could not take my eyes off the place.

I saw semis overturned and crushed in a pile. I saw houses that had been blown to pieces. I saw men and women behold their town inert and ruined, most of them in tears. Worst of all, somehow, were the images of trees that had been cut in half, like arms with their hands lopped off, reaching for the same gray sky I sat under. I read reports of old men and women crushed by the ceilings above their heads, of dogs who helped the living find the dead. I saw no corpses, but hour after hour the death toll rose.

Charlie came home a few hours early. It was a Friday, so we had the whole weekend to spend adhered to our couch, watching Cadiz. We could have driven fifteen minutes and seen the wreckage ourselves, but we thought it better to keep a respectful distance and observe from the same remove as everyone else in the country. At one point, Charlie suggested we see how we might help. "Help?" I said, and threw up my hands, as if to make plain how empty they were of lifesaving devices. Meanwhile, out the window, ambulance sirens wailed. We knew, for once, where they were going.

~

A cave cricket will sometimes get into the house. On our first morning here, the day after we moved in, I saw one crouching in the middle of what was to be our living room. I knew I would have to kill it; Charlie was out getting us coffee from a gas station.

The thing nearest my hands was an open box of some of our books. I had been lining our shelves with them. I threw a French-English dictionary at the creature. It leapt aside to safety, just a split second before the book landed. I threw another, it leapt again. I then spent ten minutes trying to kill it in this fashion. Every time—or almost every time—it saw my literature coming, it jumped out of the way. I threw *Native Son*, *Regarding the Pain of Others*, one of Charlie's old industry reports, and a Kafka anthology, before I finally crushed it with an old copy of *Dune*. I raised my arms above my head and shouted "Yes!" loudly enough to cause an echo. I announced my victory to Charlie, when he returned, with great pride. Nonplussed, he said I was acting as if I'd killed the Wicked Witch of the Midwest. The next time he went out, he returned with glue traps and put them in the corners of our rooms, to catch any creatures that landed on them and to preserve our books, he said, from ever being flung again.

The cave cricket is one of Missouri's best-kept secrets. So is the brown recluse spider—I have killed twelve of them since we moved here. Its venom is so powerful it can rot and blacken your skin with one bite; if you don't get a recluse bite treated you can lose a limb. I have heard they get in your sleeves and bite you when you put your arms through, so I shake out all of my shirts before I wear them.

The space between St. Louis and Kansas City is a death trap. Our town is at the midpoint of fatal Missouri, where if the tornadoes and fauna don't kill you, the heat will. Between May and September, the temperature is usually a hundred degrees.

I try not to complain too much to Charlie; he was equally reluctant to relocate here for his work. Mostly, I confine my grievances to conversations with my sister Anne, who is sympathetic enough from her end of the line. She has the luxury of sympathy, living back in Boston in the house where we were raised. She has yet to visit.

~

Despite the instant demolition of Cadiz, our little city went unscathed. Some trees in town lost branches, but that happens in the average thunderstorm. Some buildings were lost on Route 40, which is the quickest way to get to Cadiz, but they were outside our city limits, and our town suffered no casualties.

It hadn't even been an especially large tornado, but it hadn't needed to be because with no more than ten thousand residents, Cadiz was not a large town. It was more of a suburb, but there is no big city it could be a suburb of.

For this and other reasons, I was surprised to learn from news reports that the people of Cadiz were planning to rebuild. They didn't report this as news, per se; it was something they took for granted, saying things like, "Rebuilding has already begun," which sounds triumphant enough when spoken by a first-string newsman who has never been to Cadiz.

I wondered, having seen the relative squalor of pre-tornado Cadiz, why its people didn't simply abandon the site in favor of moving to our larger city, which, despite its many drawbacks, has sandwich shops and better schools. We have a food co-op called the Farmacy, and a vintage clothing store called Easily Suede—they had no such redeeming things in Cadiz. Many Cadizians commuted to work here in town as it was, but people get attached to their homes, and so they would restore them. In the meantime, they needed places to stay, where they could regroup as the wreckage cleared and essential things, like their hospital and grocery store, were restored to working order.

Refugees from Cadiz began arriving in our neighborhood that Monday. Community organizers—I didn't know we had them—had gone door to door all weekend, asking for volunteers to take in survivors from the dead city.

Some of our neighbors offered one or two of their rooms to those in need. A single mother two blocks down took in an orphaned toddler. The aged, retired Robinsons made an extra set of keys for a young, childless couple, no older than twenty-five, who'd lost their first house and both their jobs. A family of four settled in one bedroom in the home of some Presbyterians up the street.

We took in no one from Cadiz. It was something I talked over with Charlie, the evening of the visit of our community's organizer, an earnest man if I ever met one. He was also a bald man if I ever met one. His forehead wrinkled as he stood on the other side of our screen door, making his pitch, as the news of Cadiz blared from the TV across the room. He didn't want to guilt us into taking someone in, he said, and he could see our house was "pretty small," but he told me who had volunteered so far, and I knew some of their houses were no larger than ours. He said the survivors would only need to be here for "about a week, at most." He left me with his card, which had "Community Organizer" printed across the bottom—killing my theory, developed a minute prior, that our community had not had organizers until Cadiz was razed and people suddenly had something to do.

Charlie and I discussed it briefly, but we both knew we would never let someone else live with us. We like to be alone—with each other, but also without each other. My favorite thing about our house is that it's shaped like a U, so we can get out of each other's sight when we need to. We can each inhabit one end of the U, and with a wall between us we feel like we're by ourselves.

I knew we would make good hosts. We have two bathrooms, despite our house being "pretty small," plus an extra bedroom. But the second bedroom is my office, and the extra bathroom is where Charlie shaves every morning while I blow-dry my hair in the other one. I didn't want to give up these things, and besides, accepting a refugee would be like adopting a child. We wouldn't know we'd gotten a psychopath until it was too late.

~

Since we moved here, I have been taking morning walks with the neighbor's cat. I didn't coax him into joining me;

he followed me around the block on my first trip, and it became our routine. He slinks from bush to tree to fire hydrant as I stride over the pavement. I mostly confine these walks to my little neighborhood, which stands slightly higher than the rest of the town, kept apart from it by a four-lane road with constant, heavy traffic.

After Cadiz, when I took these walks, I would see the newest members of our modest homeless population. A bearded man who always wore the same faded, red T-shirt would sit on his borrowed porch as I went past with the cat and my travel mug full of coffee. I'd watch him from the corner of my eye, but he didn't seem to take notice. He sat alone and stared across the street, looking dazed, like he'd never seen so many houses keep still for so long.

I waved hello to some of the survivors, like an older couple who looked the way I expected a tornado's near-victims to look. It wasn't that they were permanently windblown; rather, they seemed relieved. I always knew when they were near—on my walks, at the supermarket, at the bank—because I'd hear them laughing together as they approached. They behaved as though they knew, now, that they should cherish every day they spent alive, for they recognized how precious life is in this perilous region. But as I told Charlie, I suspected this to be nothing new; they must have lived this way before the storm hit. Charlie took their good cheer as a sign that either they were very religious or had extraordinary homeowner's insurance.

Our favorite refugees were both thirty-three—a little younger than me and Charlie—and like us, they weren't from Missouri. I met them on one of my walks with the neighbor's cat. I had just passed the house with the bewildered man on the porch when there came my way a man and woman both dressed in jeans and T-shirts. The man was tall—at least six foot two—the woman half a foot shorter. They had brown hair and brown eyes. They looked younger than they turned out to be. As I neared them, I didn't let on that I'd noticed them, and they did the same. As we got closer, we made eye contact, all of us squinting as if we knew each other from somewhere. As soon as we passed, I turned to say hello. They returned the greeting, and as we stopped walking in opposite directions I said, "My name's Karen," and they introduced themselves as Claire and Jared. I asked, "Are you all from Cadiz?" pronouncing it as the Cadizians do, diplomatically. They nodded and turned around and walked with me for several blocks as we talked. They didn't have a destination, they said, it was just that they had been taking morning walks in Cadiz and didn't want to give up the habit simply because their town had ceased to exist. I could tell they were realistic people. They said they were staying in the neighborhood, and I invited them over that evening, "for drinks."

They came, and together we had a night like I hadn't had since moving to Missouri, one in which you get to know someone with the fullest confidence that you're going to like them as much, if not more, when the evening ends as you did when it started. We sat on our screened-in porch, under the moon and the sound of crickets of the aboveground variety.

Jared was from outside Seattle. Claire was born in Minnesota. Jared and I had the same number of friends as teenagers who eventually died from heroin overdoses; he said it was not uncommon in a place like Seattle, and I said it was "a Boston thing, too." Jared, we learned, liked beer, enough that he and Charlie followed the same beer blogs. Claire shared my love-hate relationship with cooking, in that we both liked the idea of cooking but didn't like to wait for things to heat up—which, said Claire, is at least seventy percent of cooking. I felt as blessed by their company as

143

they must have felt cursed, considering they'd just lost their house and their dog. He had been a Weimaraner, one who went by the unlikely name of Fat Joe. They both cried a little when they mentioned this, and I think Jared drank at least two more of Charlie's IPAs than he would have had they not suffered such a loss a few days before.

I was surprised to see them cry; I had been struck by how the storm hadn't seemed to faze them. Claire said they'd mostly felt guilty about "the whole thing." They had not been harmed or known anyone who had. "It was scary," Jared said. "Really scary, I mean"—but, he explained, they had just moved to Cadiz a week before. Most of their furniture was still on its way, by freight, to the rubble that had been their rented house—which, added Claire, they hadn't even liked very much.

Claire's tears had come as abruptly as the cyclone, and Jared's followed. I considered reaching across to Claire, putting my hand on her shoulder to comfort her, but despite our moderate social lubrication, I didn't know if I knew her well enough to do that. A few minutes later, they said they should get going. They said their host family might worry if they didn't, and so they went.

Perhaps I should have gone through with the hand-to-shoulder contact, I thought in days to follow. I asked Charlie the next morning if I had done something wrong, if I hadn't been responsive enough to Claire's tears. Some people know exactly what to do when someone else in a room begins to cry. I am not one of them. When we didn't hear from them, Charlie maintained that they probably weren't ignoring us on purpose. They had, he said, things on their minds that were bigger than me.

~

If you looked at certain websites in the weeks after Cadiz, you would never have guessed that a tornado seized the town and emptied it out. On the Cadiz Craigslist page, life carried on. Men, as before, were looking for love, or looking for casual sex, or looking to sell their motorcycles. Women were doing things, too. When announcing furniture for sale, no one mentioned the weather pattern that may or may not have torn the roof from over their heads. The single men weren't looking for replacements for the wives they'd just lost—though when I brought this up with Charlie, he said that if this were the case it was the sort of detail likely to be left out of a three-sentence Craigslist ad.

Eerier to me was how the town looked on Google's Street View feature. Touring Cadiz on Google was like traveling one week back in time. According to Google, the courthouse was still standing. The hospital was whole, the trees had their leaves and weren't broken in half, and although the sandwich shops were missing, they hadn't been there before the tornado either. I knew—and Charlie reminded me—that this should not have seemed strange. Google doesn't update its street views on a biweekly basis. Still, on some level I expect a street to look in life the way it looks online. I know I am not alone in this, even if Charlie isn't with me.

I returned to Cadiz often, through Google, retracing the steps I took on my one visit there in person. I skipped my walk with the neighbor's cat on some mornings, in favor of my virtual stroll through the now-missing city. I googled my way past Granny's Gifts, an antique shop, where a woman held a door for a man, both of them frozen in place. Next, on my right, were the coffeehouse and post office. They weren't there anymore, but there they were.

I could see people at the wheels of their cars and on the sidewalk. At least one of them must have been recently killed. I kept my virtual walks carefully hidden from Charlie, who, if he had caught me taking them, would have made a remark he thought was very funny.

Near as Cadiz was, and even after much of the wreckage had supposedly been cleared, I was not about to drive there and see the ex-town for myself, despite the curiosity that kept me coming back to pictures of it in ruins. I had spent so much time thinking about Cadiz, and watching it, without venturing in, that to go there now would have been embarrassing, like breaking a deeply uncomfortable silence with an ex-friend who has become a virtual stranger.

~

Two weeks after our evening of drinks together, we heard again from Claire and Jared. They e-mailed to say they were living in a FEMA trailer beside the wreckage of their rented house, which would soon be cleared by a construction crew, to make room for the next incarnation of their rented house. They said that to access the Internet they had to drive five miles to the nearest Starbucks. They asked if we wanted to meet again.

We did, and while I never went so far as to establish these terms for our friendship, I would spend time with them as long as it meant not going to Cadiz. On a Sunday, we lent them our extra pair of bikes and went for a ride on the Mason Trail. One Saturday afternoon, we took a long drive that ended at the winery on the river, which I was especially glad to do because driving west for twenty minutes to reach it meant getting even farther from Cadiz.

Jared and Claire spent almost none of our time together talking about the tornado that had murdered Fat Joe and

146

two hundred Cadizians. They never volunteered their tale of surviving the storm, and we never asked for it, but they did mention some things they had lost. They waxed nostalgic, not traumatic, as we discussed pre-cyclonic Cadiz. Claire said that although she hadn't been glad to relocate from Philadelphia for the sake of Jared's job, she'd seen some good in the town. They'd had a surprisingly active ceramics scene, she said, though that was gone now.

The thing she missed most was her car. It had been her first car and it had "run just fine" even after all those years of owning it—how many years she didn't say. Now she didn't know where it was. It was probably in a field somewhere, I submitted, to which she nodded, looking away.

More to my liking, our new friends volunteered objections to Missouri as a whole. The way we talked, one would think tornadoes were the least of its problems. Jared said there was a kind of tree they had in Philadelphia—he couldn't say what kind—that he didn't see here. Missing it made him feel like he was "in a foreign country." Claire complained how hard it was to find a decent cup of coffee, a comment that prompted the rest of us to nod vigorously in agreement.

Typically quiet in conversation, this subject matter animated me. I live just a thousand miles from the place I call home, I said, but it feels like not another country but another planet. "There's nothing I recognize here," I said. "The buildings don't look right. It's all so new."

Claire asked, "How old is the oldest building? Not even two hundred years, right?"

Empowered, I told the three of them about the long walk I took the day Cadiz was crushed. I had not yet mentioned it to Charlie, or to anyone else.

I was visited, on the morning of Cadiz's ruin, by a cave cricket. Claire groaned at my mention of it. It was the biggest one I'd ever seen, I said. It was the boldest one, too. Out of nowhere it landed on my desk, so that I leapt backward, sending my chair hurtling to the floor. I knew at once that my workday was over. I knew if I left for a while and came back later it would make itself scarce, creeping under a dresser or behind the stove, sparing me the ordeal of trying to kill it, so I put on my sandals and ventured out.

I had also just had a long talk with Anne, who told me a walk might make me feel better about living here. "Missouri is one of the least polluted states in the country," she said, making this information up. "Breathe the air."

The cat joined me, as usual, but I veered from our typical course to head into town. My feline companion stopped and crept home behind me when I left our niche with its garages and cultivated greenery. I had no destination. There was nothing I wanted to buy. There weren't even nice-looking buildings to see, not like back home, where if I walked in any direction for five minutes, I'd at least see an old church to make my trip worth the trouble. Jared nodded at this.

It was mid-morning, and I got as far as the littered four-lane highway, where a man stood at the crosswalk. Despite his location, and the way he looked expectantly out at the cars, he didn't want to cross the street. Many of the drivers thought he did, as they waited through the first half of every green light to let him go. They watched him as the light changed and continued to watch him after it did. Then, his lack of intention made plain, they drove on, shaking their heads or raising their hands, palms up in disbelief and fury. They'd been faked out, and throughout it he stood perfectly still, with his round glasses and pink baseball cap.

I don't think he knew he was the cause of this confusion and anger. He looked oblivious, which is how he has looked

148

every other time I've seen him. In the daytime, and at night, he wanders through town asking strangers for money, maintaining his characteristic, incongruous expression, not unlike the look of someone who is hard at work on a crossword puzzle. He'll approach and ask, slurring, if we've "got any change," but whereas the average panhandler on the East Coast will put some life into his pitch and claim that he merely needs change for bus fare, or something, this man asks for it as if he's not sure what money is and wants only to hold some to see how much it weighs.

I could sense that my friends expected this story to have a climax, so I pushed on: there is something about this part of the country that seems to cultivate pointless, dull oddities like this man. "He wouldn't last five minutes in Boston," I said. "Here he's part of the landscape." It was the landscape I found fault with, I explained, not the man—this place without topography, this infernal land that hills forgot.

I told them how I'd looked out at all the cars stopped in traffic and the gray buildings and wondered why any of it was ever put there. I wondered how it was not smashed to pieces long before, and as my friends and husband listened, I gathered from the gathering clouds that were their expressions that I had ventured into territory where they would not follow. "It's not that I wished a tornado on Cadiz," I said, looking at Claire's unsmiling face. "I wouldn't wish that on anybody."

And I would never say, I explained, that God had punished the people of Cadiz for anything. "I don't believe in God. But I wonder if—you know—we should take this last tornado as a sign that maybe there are better places to live."

Perhaps my story went over so poorly because we were at the winery, and the wine was okay, and the day was pretty, with the river glittering behind me where I couldn't see it, but the others could. The others were looking at the scenery that stretched away from us. I had cast an awkward pall. I knew I could do one of two things: either dig myself a deeper hole or shut up. Eventually someone praised the wine and we moved on.

I had not told them how, when I got home, the cave cricket had not crept into a hole at all. He was in plain sight, caught in one of Charlie's glue traps. All six of his legs and both antennae were stuck to the surface. He would never come unstuck; to pull him away would have killed him. Cave crickets don't make noise, so he stood there looking lifeless, but very much alive. I didn't know what to do. I wanted to end his life for him, but anything I crushed him with would stick to the trap, and the glue might never come off. I didn't want to throw the trap out. I didn't want to go near him. So I left him there, and I kept an eye on him all that day, and on the day to follow, as he slowly, helplessly died.

~

I still have not ventured into Cadiz, but I think about it often, even though I've half-forgotten the earthquake in Haiti and other tornadoes south of us. It's not because Cadiz is so close, for it might as well be in Pakistan for all the contact I've had with it and all but two of its people. There is something else involved, something more than morbid curiosity, I told Charlie when he caught me watching Cadiz clips on YouTube six months after the storm and asked why I still paid it such attention.

I didn't tell him what it is, and he didn't ask. It is fear, but not a fear I am used to. It is like a new kind of fear someone at Google invented, a fear I never knew until I moved to Missouri. It stems from the constant threat of tornadoes, but has more to do with these empty landscapes, the Missouri license plates I am still not used to seeing everywhere, and the way our house makes me feel, when I am in it, like I am still outside, no matter what part of the house I am in.

And there is more to it even than that. In those first weeks after the storm, when I looked at images of Cadiz, I felt, in a small way, validated. It was as if my inward impression of Cadiz and its outward appearance had, in the space of a few minutes, been reconciled. Cadiz was so irresistible to me after the storm because finally one piece of Missouri looked to everyone else the way it had appeared to me all along.

I would not have admitted that at the time—not even for the purpose of creating awkward moments at wineries. It is the kind of thing Charlie would not understand, and I don't think anyone else would get it either, at least not anyone who lives around here.

Gunmen

Had I known the gunman was on his way, had I known what I was dreaming when I dreamt his arrival in advance, I would have prepared for his coming. I'd have stashed an extra gun in the desk at the front of the room and ensured that the students knew it was there. I would have planted a claymore at the entrance to the classroom, just above the door. I would have rigged a steel trap that might have kept the gunman from bringing any harm to the students I was meant to keep safe.

Better yet: I would have told the students not to come in that day. Had I known not only that he would come, but when, I would have cancelled my class and saved the lives of nine people.

Damn the evaluation forms they had to fill out. Damn the whole college, and the rotten country that knew how likely it was that the gunman would come but didn't stand in his way, did nothing to stop him. Rather than stop him, they ensured his access to arms and armor, like gods outfitting Theseus for a task much less sensible than the slaying of a Minotaur.

It would have made sense to slay a Minotaur. It would have made more sense, anyway, than it did for the gunman to slay all the students enrolled in the course in World Literature that it was up to me to teach, that spring semester, at the little college where I had been a professor for just under one decade.

I was teaching only the one class that semester, and most it went on without the interference of any gunmen.

I knew he was out there. He was always out there. Every teacher knows he is out there and pictures often the scene of his entrance and the end of everything. I had to be on my guard, and I was, but still I didn't really think he would ever come for me and the kids on my roster. We all know we will die, eventually, but we spend most of our waking lives not acknowledging it, not thinking about it. Instead we do things like teach classes on World Literature, like I was doing, one morning, in my teaching posture, sitting on the edge of the desk with my hands folded in what passed for my lap, since I wasn't fully sitting down. I had on my blue plaid suit, one of three I ordered at a discount from a catalog.

My eyes were closed, as they often were when I addressed a classroom full of students. I squinted and the squint built until my eyes were all but shut. It wasn't because I was shy; I'm not shy. It wasn't because I was daunted by the size of the crowd in there, as there were only nine students. It was simply one of the habits one takes on when becoming a teacher, one of the things you don't expect you'll ever do, until the time comes to address groups of youngfolk several times a week on subjects that don't interest them. Adopting new behaviors that don't make sense is part of the job.

By that point in the semester, they had worked their way through Cormac McCarthy's early career as an Appalachian novelist. I was lecturing now on *Blood Meridian*. A discussion would follow, but I like to lay the conversational foundation with a mini-lecture at the start of every meeting.

Lecture is too strong a word. Even mini-lecture is too strong. I was just talking. I hadn't read the novel in a while, and the notes I was working from were bare-bones.

The students didn't know that. They didn't care. They had given up. They had lost faith in the class four weeks prior, when Phillip—brave Phillip—took it upon himself to complain openly that I was not teaching the class properly.

I don't know what you mean, I said, with my attempt at a winning, inviting smile.

It's World Literature, said Phillip. I mean, it's supposed to be. That's what we signed up for. But all we're reading are Cormac McCarthy novels.

You knew that, though, from day one, I said with the index finger of my left hand in the air. It's on the syllabus. I read you the syllabus.

Phillip looked away.

It still doesn't make sense, said Addison, from the other side of the classroom. Cormac McCarthy isn't World Literature.

It is, though. Again I smiled. I cleared my throat. What is our world all about? What's it made of?

Silence.

Borders, I said. Our world is borders. It's refugees who are desperate to cross them. It's fanatics with guns who refuse to let them cross. The modern world is all about borders, and McCarthy's novels are about crossing them. The characters go back and forth, across borders. You need look no further than McCarthy to find World Literature.

But that's not the point, said Phillip. It's not the point of this class. Right?

What do you mean?

World Literature is supposed to be about the literature of the world. You take the class and read stuff from, like, Namibia. And South America.

And China, said Gary from the back of the room, which was where Gary sat. He was leaning forward, which is the opposite of how he's usually leaning.

I know what you're saying, I said, my palms upraised. You heard about how other people teach this class and thought that's what this one would be. But not all professors have a uniform approach.

Phillip leaned back and looked away significantly. No one spoke for a moment.

Give it some time, I said. *Child of God* (the novel we were then reading) is probably McCarthy's most isolated novel. Wait until we get to *Blood Meridian*. We'll revisit this.

Now, though, it was four weeks later, and we were on *Blood Meridian*. I had no desire to revisit that conversation, to talk again about how the novels of Cormac McCarthy are all the world literature anyone needs. I don't think Phillip wanted to discuss it again, either.

I told them about the echoes of *Moby-Dick* that are so apparent in *Blood Meridian*, the way in which in *Blood Meridian* you have, as in *Moby-Dick*, a protagonist who is swept up by forces much greater than himself, represented by a band of men who decide his fate for him. He observes them as we, the readers, look over his shoulder. I talked about the historical referents for *Blood Meridian*, and asked them what, in the writing of the novel, made it plain that the narrative hinged on some corresponding historical record.

They said nothing. None looked in my direction, for fear of making eye contact.

Making eye contact with a professor, or at least with me, was for students at this college like making eye contact with a scary bear, except that where the bear might rear up and maul the students I was likely to take their eye contact as an indication that something was happening behind their eyes.

There might be neurons firing there, and they might like to contribute to what I would want to call a discussion but what was really a reluctant monologue.

I let the silence hang over the room for half a minute before volunteering that we could discern a kind of mock veracity in the way the events of the novel play out, the way it is paced. When McCarthy has the novel trudge along the way it does, with significant events mixed with insignificant events, indiscriminately, in a perfectly linear fashion, it makes the narrative seem more real. It makes it plain that McCarthy is anchoring his imagination to a historical record. If the narrative didn't do that, if it jumped around in time, without warning, that sense of veracity would be compromised. We would be lost in something else, like the loose structure of a character's active mind, to have a strong sense of correspondence between the fiction at hand and historical reality. There might still be some truth to it, I said. The narrative might still be telling us something. Maybe something not unlike what *Blood Meridian* has to say. But it would take a different shape.

None of this mattered to the students. They didn't care.

It was time to go, and I said so.

As the students filed out, I secured my sidearm, buttoning it into the holster that rested under my left arm. I hadn't taken it out of its holster, but I liked, during class, to keep the little strap unbuttoned, so that if I needed to use it, I could access it more readily.

I don't want to suggest that I had an interest in murdering Phillip, nor that I thought I might have to defend myself against him. He could be a problem student, sure, but that was no reason to end his life. He wasn't a threat. And I am no cold-blooded killer.

It wasn't Phillip who worried me. It was the killers who worried me, the real killers: the guys who want nothing more than to shoot up a school like mine with an AR-15, or maybe two of them, or an AR-15 and a shotgun, more likely an AR-15, a shotgun, and a couple of pistols. The killers at schools bring as many guns as they can, so they don't have to reload. Instead of reloading, they switch guns. They murder by the dozens and take their own lives. It's old news.

I walked behind my single-file students as they made their way to their cars in the parking lot. Some of them were headed to other classes. Bella lived in a dormitory, so she went that-a-way, but for a while we went in the same direction, and so I kept one eye on them all as I scanned the vicinity—the windows of nearby classroom buildings, and the parking lot—for threats.

I didn't see any threats.

I did see Daniel.

I think they've got it from here, said Daniel.

I'm just looking out, I said, nodding, squinting again. Daniel was my department chair.

He asked how I was. I'm fine, I said. Tired, I said. Tired is all.

Daniel nodded and said what I expected him to say: that there had been another complaint about the class I was teaching.

You mean 326?

Uh-huh.

Same problem?

Yeah.

I guess—what? Three students have complained, now?

That's right.

We laughed our uneasy laughs, standing there in our coats, our guns under our jackets and coats.

Daniel's gun was a Smith & Wesson Model 41. A .22 caliber semiautomatic, with a carbon steel frame and carbon steel slide, it was a top-of-the-line rimfire pistol with an adjustable rear sight and a partridge on the front. It wasn't exactly the pistol of choice for college professors. It was more of a recreational pistol, a sport shooter's pistol. But it could still bring down an active shooter. It still used bullets. The dean had approved it, on those grounds.

Daniel was a gun guy. He had a lot of guns at home—I'd seen them—and he saw the requirement that he carry a gun, legislated five years prior, as a chance to do two things he had wanted to do: have a gun on him when he was on campus, and acquire yet another gun. He chose the S&W Model 41 as his campus gun, he said, in a long conversation we had at the time, mostly because he didn't have one yet. With a Miller Light in his hand, at his house, he made it sound like he was putting one over on the school, taking advantage of them, seizing the opportunity to get the school to help him grow his gun collection. Whatever.

I had a harder time picking out a gun than Daniel did. I didn't know anything about guns.

Plus, I don't like shopping in general. I don't care if it's a different kind of shopping, from the usual kind, where the gun vendors come to campus once a year and set up tables in the basement of the English department building and hock their wares to the faculty. It doesn't matter to me that I'm not spending my own money, that the school buys us the guns that we're required by law to keep under our jackets or on the smalls of our backs, in ankle holsters or on automatic sliding rigs strapped to our arms like Travis Bickle.

Daniel was overjoyed on the day of the first campus gun fair. He positively vibrated with gun enthusiasm. He didn't smile, but he moved with a sense of purpose I didn't, at the time, associate with Daniel.

He insisted on helping me find the right gun. I told him I was all right, I didn't need help. He followed me around anyway. He followed for twenty minutes, as I picked up guns and looked at them, and asked questions of the vendors that I knew Daniel must have thought were bad questions. I remember I asked the Glock guy why the company was called Glock. I don't remember his answer.

It was at the Ruger table that, at last, I found the gun for me.

There it was, lying on a white tablecloth. It looked like an old friend. It reminded me of Elliot, my friend from the private school I attended in Pennsylvania, when I was young.

Elliot always looked like he was not in his rightful place. Even in his parents' living room, where we would watch television, he seemed not to belong. His teeth didn't fit in his face. His legs were too short for his body.

The Ruger SP101 Double-Action Revolver had a handle that seemed too short for the rest of its body. But then it felt just right in my hand. The feel of my finger curling around the trigger was something like the feeling of pulling on a snug winter glove. I even laughed for a second, at the way it fit cold and small in my hand.

The SP101 carried five rounds, one in each chamber. This one was a .38 Special, said the vendor, with a solid stainless-steel frame. It had a smooth double-action trigger pull—hence the name—with an understated front sight that made drawing it from my holster a cinch. Just above and to the right of the trigger it had an R with a circle around it, meaning "restricted."

Which endeared me to it even more. This was a gun that was careful about trademark violations.

I said to the sales guy, I'll take this one.

Sure thing, he said. He said it would be delivered to me at my department in a month.

Daniel stopped me. Are you sure you want that gun? he said.

Yeah, I said.

You're sure.

Sure.

You know how many bullets that holds?

No.

Five.

Okay.

Suppose you miss five times.

I turned to him, now, with the gun in my palm. You think I should get one with six bullets?

I think you should get one with ten.

I shook my head. No, I said. I like this one.

You do.

I nodded.

You don't think you should get a semi-automatic? One that's less likely to jam?

I shook my head.

Listen, he said. You can't let nostalgia get in the way of your professional obligation.

I shrugged. I'm not nostalgic about guns, I said. I don't really care about guns.

But you want that one.

That's right.

Enough to spend extra time working on your aim?

At the range?

Yes. At the range.

I stood my ground. Yes, I said.

Okay, said Daniel. As soon as this bad boy comes in, I want you down there four hours a week.

It hadn't always been this way. Mine hadn't always been a profession in which a department chair could tell an Associate Professor how much time he had to spend at the campus shooting range. It hadn't always been one in which a professor could hijack a World Literature course and teach only Cormac McCarthy novels in it.

I didn't know what to tell Daniel about my class, which a third of the students had now gone to him to complain about.

I shrugged. Daniel shrugged, too.

You can't win them all, he said. Take it as a lesson and learn from it.

I'll do that, I said. I nodded, and Daniel did what he does when he doesn't feel like saying more things. He walked away without saying goodbye, leaving me to gather that the conversation was over.

I went to my office, on the third floor of Glock Hall, my feet reverberating down the hardwood hall, echoing in and out of empty offices.

It's one thing I always liked about the college, or at least about the building that housed the English Department. Every year, they promised to renovate the building, to carpet floors and replace light switches. And whatever else they would have done. Every year, though, the funding came up short. The school must have spent all of its annual budget buying guns for its faculty and staff, keeping the shooting range staffed and stocked with ammunition, and fueling the school helicopter that could be heard circling overhead from time to time.

I don't know. I loved that they never went through with the renovation. I love hardwood floors. My two favorite things are metal and wood.

It used to be that I shared an office, but I didn't have to share it anymore. There had been fifteen offices on the third floor, and twenty-two full-time faculty to use them. But when Teach and Carry passed, and the President (of the United States, not the college) didn't veto it, nearly the whole department abandoned ship, all but eight of us, which meant there were offices to spare. Seven of them.

A college abhors a vacuum, and so they put those offices to use as storage areas for obsolete computers and office furniture. There weren't people in the offices because the college administrators opted not to replace the full-time faculty who resigned when Teach and Carry was signed into law. They hired adjunct instructors, which aren't the same thing.

Because no one new was in the offices, just mostly old Macintosh computers, the whole third floor felt like it was haunted, like the offices were waiting for the departed faculty to return.

They never would. Drs. Cohen and McIntyre were long gone. Once, they worked down the hall, but now they were doing other things with their lives. I didn't know what.

Gary Glower was gone—I think he went to law school. I think he was young enough to start over. Donald Justice wasn't young enough, at least not in his own eyes; he overdosed on sleeping pills and died a month after he quit.

Amy Gerstler, who also jumped ship but didn't kill herself, cried at the emergency department meeting that convened the day after Teach and Carry passed.

Paul James cried after the meeting, in his office. I could hear him through the wooden wall that stood between us.

I didn't like Teach and Carry any more than the others did, but unlike most of them I wasn't willing to quit my job over it. I had worked too hard to get the job. I had gone to college, gone to grad school for two years, gone to more grad school for five more years, then spent three years on a difficult job market before finally landing this position. I had found my calling and pursued my calling like it was itself a full-time job.

Plus, I never thought I'd have to use the gun.

I knew it could happen. It happened all the time, that teachers had to put their sidearms to use. There were lots of school shootings, and I had no reason to think they would stop for me. I lived in constant fear of them, in fact. But still I could not picture myself in the line of fire.

And I didn't mind having to wear a gun. It was, in fact, the fact that I wore it that actually made it appealing.

Not long before the Teach and Carry bill passed and stipulated that I had to have a gun at school, I had started wearing a suit and tie when I taught. Before, I wore regular pants and dress shirts. But I decided it was time for a change, when I turned 35. It was time to dress like a man who was 35. I ordered some suits by way of catalogs and bought ties. It didn't matter that no other 35-year-old men dressed in those things anymore; it was how I thought I should dress, now that I'd reached the middle of my fourth decade.

Suddenly I had choices to make in the morning, things to adorn myself with that weren't just a shirt and pants. I didn't merely get dressed every day; I had to put an *outfit* together. I could wear a tie clip, or not wear a tie clip. I had several belts to choose from. There were colors to coordinate.

A gun with its holster were more than another couple of clothing accessories. They were much more than that. But putting on my gun soon became another step in the daily process of suiting up. The new accessories went well with the old ones. They fit together in a way I did not expect.

Then, soon after the mass exodus of most of the rest of the faculty, I was promoted to Associate Professor. I was granted tenure, which would not have happened had the exodus not taken place.

Suddenly, they couldn't throw a small fish back anymore, with only me and seven other guys left in the department. It didn't matter that I'd never been popular with students. No one cared anymore that my research had mostly been insightless fanboy stuff about Kurt Vonnegut and William Gibson.

I'll admit here what I could not admit before, for professional reasons: I had little to nothing of substance to say about anything, at least when it comes to books.

It was half the reason I was teaching the Cormac McCarthy class, or teaching the World Literature class as a Cormac McCarthy class. It was there that I sought a remedy for my problem of not having compelling ideas to speak about with passion at conferences. I thought if I had real conversations with young people about McCarthy's novels, I'd come out of them with something to write. I was slated to present at the annual McCarthy conference some months later, and so I had to have something ready by then, something to say.

Okay. That's not true.

I didn't really need to have anything to say. If I didn't, I would read a substance-free paper to the assembled professors and embarrass myself, then come back the next year and do the same thing. It's what I did every year at the annual meeting of the Kurt Vonnegut Society, and I did it once on a Thomas Pynchon panel. There were no consequences then, either.

But I wanted to do more than that, this time. I wanted to make an impression. Teaching a class on Cormac McCarthy was my way of making it happen. I would be put in circumstances where I had to talk at length about

McCarthy's books. I was likely to say something interesting, eventually. Or a student would, and I would use that.

It's not alchemy, writing a sufficient conference paper. It's not like I didn't have a Ph.D.

It's not as if McCarthy hasn't written some of the strangest and most profound novels of the last half-century. And I haven't failed to notice some of the elements that animated those novels with significance.

There was, for example, the way McCarthy owed so much to Charles Brockden Brown, Gothic novelist of the early nineteenth century, and author of *Wieland*, which resembles in remarkable ways McCarthy's *Outer Dark*.

In both novels—both of them American gothic novels— you have a brother and sister who are left to fend for themselves in an inhospitable, otherworldly America. In both novels, the brother and sister are separated. The villain of each novel, who is revealed to be the villain only at the very end, is a calm, eloquent psychopath, who kills people without having a compelling reason to do so, as if he can't help himself. The bad guy at the end of *Outer Dark*, who does terrible things (including murder) to a small child, might as well be Carwin the Biloquist, from *Wieland*, who inspires a different guy (Wieland) to murder several small children.

A side note: the villain in *Outer Dark* is remarkably like the Misfit in Flannery O'Connor's *A Good Man is Hard to Find*. It's really remarkable how similar they are. Both are horribly cruel; both seem to have things figured out in ways that don't align with a morality acceptable to anyone else.

I told all this to attendees at the first McCarthy conference I attended, but they appeared nonplussed. When my panel was over, no one asked me any questions. There were lots of questions for another man on the panel, who had a big beard, and had a much bigger gun than I did, the

166

handle of which I could see sticking out of his jacket from where I sat. It must have been a .44.

Look at *Blood Meridian* and *Edgar Huntly*, I had told the same audience just prior to the lively Q&A in which I did not participate. Both books are gothic novels that feature Native Americans as forces of nature, disembodied threats that appear in the form of arrows that fly or have recently flown at white people.

You can see Brockden Brown's influence all over McCarthy's work, I assured them.

I didn't have much to say, other than to point that out.

I guess it wasn't a very good paper. I suppose I should have spent more time on it. Probably not.

In my office, I hung up my blazer and shoulder holster, gun still inside, on the coatrack by the door.

When the professors first got our guns, we had a hard time taking them seriously. I used to have standoffs with Gerald, the literary theory guy. We would draw and pull our triggers, like they do in westerns, only we took the bullets out of our guns first. That was what made it fun to us, the fact that we couldn't kill each other or any bystanders, since the guns were empty. It wouldn't have been funny, otherwise.

We stopped doing it when one morning a student emerged from the stairwell into the hallway where we did this, right into our crossfire, and, looking one way and another, began screaming and crying. She dropped to the floor and wailed and howled. We were stunned.

No one emerged from the other offices. No one was in them.

It turned out, this poor student's brother had been shot and paralyzed for life a few years prior, at a college campus in Vermont. He had enrolled there because he didn't think there would be gun massacres at schools in Vermont.

With my gun hanging from the coatrack, it felt like
something was missing from my body, like I'd taken out
one of my more essential bones and hung it there. I spent so
much time with the gun under my arm, it didn't feel right
when it wasn't there. I felt lighter without it. I was lighter,
without it. My particular one wasn't so heavy, but guns are
heavy in general. They're metal. All day long I could feel
the weight of it pulling at my shoulder. I was self-conscious
about it, even after I got used to its constant mass.

It wasn't a problem for me to take the gun home, because
I lived alone. My girlfriend left me soon after I started
bringing the gun home at night.

It wasn't the gun that bothered her, she said. It was the
way my personality changed after I got it.

What are you talking about, I said.

She tried to explain: I walked differently, now that I had
the gun. When I entered a room, I scanned it for threats,
where before I had not scanned for threats. She could tell by
the way my eyes moved across a given space that that was
what I was doing—looking for doors and other ways an
attacker might get in, looking for suspicious characters,
whatever that might mean in a given situation.

I talked in my sleep about the gunman, she said. Who is
the gunman? she had asked many times.

I had explained who he was, many times.

I'd said the gunman was the man who might well emerge
someday from the hallway into my classroom with a
shotgun and take the life of everyone in there, one by one.
He would probably start with me, knowing I was the
teacher, because of the way I dressed and how much older I
was than the students. He would know that I was armed
and eliminate me first.

With me bleeding out on the floor, he would line the
others against the wall and put a bullet in each of their

brains, like the man who attacked the Amish school, where the older girls volunteered to be murdered first, after he may or may not have raped some of them. Reports aren't clear.

The gunman was coming, I told Shirley. He would find me if I stayed at the college long enough. He might be listening to music on his headphones, turned up loud to drown out my begging and the students' screams.

He might be a student in one of my classes. He might be a stranger, someone who was shooting up a school because he knew there would be more easy targets there than anyplace else.

Where else can you go, I asked Shirley, on more than one occasion, to find a lot of people who've trapped themselves in rooms that have one exit?

Shirley didn't like when I talked like this. I was using my teacher voice. I was giving her a lecture. She was my girlfriend, and I should not have tried to give her a lecture.

Say you're a suicidal killer, I said, and you want the highest body count possible. Where do you go, to kill more people than you can at any other place?

Not a hospital. There are lots of exits in a hospital, and only a few people in every room, at most. There's security there, and they've got guns. That's a deterrent.

A bigger deterrent, though, is the access to exits you have in a hospital that you don't want your victims to have. People run when they're scared. You don't want them to have a place to run.

Office buildings are out, too. They have exits, and partitions, and places to hide. Movie theaters work, but they aren't usually crowded, because there are no good movies anymore, and people are afraid of getting gun-massacred at theaters. They're afraid to die in schools, but they still go to schools. They're required to, up to a point, and it's hard to get by without a college degree, so there are people in those buildings.

If you're the gunman, you know every school has a long hallway with lots of doors on either side. Through each door there are maybe thirty people sitting there, four or five floors up sometimes. That high up, they can't escape through the window. They can't save themselves. If you bring enough bullets, they have no choice but to die.

There's at least one school in every town. You're never far from a school.

And do you think, asked Shirley, that having a gun protects you from that? From a killer who has bigger guns than you? Wearing body armor?

No, I said. My gun won't protect me. I'm more likely to wound the gunman with my gun than to kill him, and a wounded gunman can still kill people.

Exits would protect you from him, said Shirley.

What? I said.

It just seems to me, she said, that the real problem is, you have nowhere to run, at the school. In your classroom. More doorways and staircases would save your life, if a gunman came for you. Or fire escapes. If you could run, you could save yourself, and your students could save themselves.

But school buildings aren't made with more than one or two exits and there are no ladders out the windows, or fire escapes.

Why not change jobs? she said. You could switch careers. It's not too late for that.

I shrugged. I like being a professor, I said. I'll do what I have to do to keep being one.

Even that? said Shirley, pointing at the gun I'd left on the table.

Yeah, I said. Even that.

There wasn't anything abrupt about our breakup. It must have taken a couple of months, and we didn't shout. Shirley didn't storm out of my place with her toothbrush and the clothes she'd kept there. Instead, we reached a stage where it was clear the end was coming, like our coupling was a book we'd been reading, and we had both looked ahead to see there weren't many pages left. After a certain point, with maybe a month left, every time she came over, she took something of hers back with her.

I know why she did it, and why we split up. It wasn't that I had my gun. That didn't matter so much. The problem was that the gun came to seem like a part of my body.

It wasn't that I talked so often about the gunman who I feared would come for me at the school. It was the way my voice changed when I talked about him, the way I made him real by referring to him, as if by referring to him as often as I did, I summoned him.

The way I talked about him changed as I learned to better wield the pistol I carried. On occasion I would boast, half-joking, to Shirley, that if he came for me and my students, I would stop him in his tracks.

I was not being reasonable. She told me so. I brushed her off.

When Shirley left, she took the electric mixer she had lent me indefinitely. She'd had two of them—God knows why she'd had two of them—so that when she left me at last, I had to go out and buy another mixer. I didn't intend to mix anything. I just liked having it there. The kitchen seemed empty without one—something like the way I felt, on the one day I forgot to take my gun to school with me, like part of my body was missing.

It was the day when we'd read the first part of *All the Pretty Horses* and were to discuss it in class.

I don't like the way this guy uses words, said Riley the boy. I don't like his words, he said.

This statement outed him as having read nothing else all semester, because McCarthy had been using words the same way in all of the other novels we'd read.

I didn't like the violence in the last novel, said Alison, meaning *Blood Meridian*, though she could have meant any McCarthy novel. Even *Suttree*. And I get that there's going to be more of it in this one, she said. And I don't like that.

I agree with that, said Phillip. I still think about that part with the babies' heads exploding. It makes me sick, when I think about it.

He was talking about a scene in *Blood Meridian*, in which two babies' heads explode. As he talked, I considered telling the class my infant mortality rate theory.

My infant mortality rate theory was something I started writing, but didn't finish, when I was in grad school. The theory went that if you looked at the years that McCarthy published a novel, you would see a spike in the infant mortality rate in those same years. I wanted to connect the way babies keep dying in his novels to some reality outside of his novels. I didn't want to suggest that the novels' publication inspired the deaths of babies, only that there might be a correlation. I wrote ten pages of that paper, but then, when I started looking into infant mortality rates, I found that my argument had no substance and didn't make sense.

I declined to mention any of this to the students, which was one of the smart decisions I made that semester.

Whenever we started discussing a new McCarthy novel, in the World Literature class, after I mini-lectured a little, I let the students complain for a while, pointing out the things they didn't like. There were always things they didn't like. I let them vent, so that we could then get on with the real talk.

It didn't work. It worked in other classes I taught, in which the gesture let the students know that their thoughts were welcome, that their gut reactions to what we read mattered and had a place in our discussions. But it didn't work with these students. There was nothing they had to say that came after the two minutes of hateful conversation. They hated everything I put in front of them, without exception, and that's all they wanted to talk about.

I addressed their concerns. I took them seriously, but also deflected them. The reason *Blood Meridian* was so violent, I said, is that the American frontier was violent. Empire-building is violent. People killed real babies, on the frontier. If McCarthy left that out, it would be beyond dishonest. I thought that would settle the question, but no.

They didn't want to let *Blood Meridian* go. Pygmalion said she thought the woman chained by her neck like a dog was too much and that she couldn't sleep at night since reading that part.

A pregnant silence ensued.

This is the novel McCarthy wrote, though, I said. And it's just a novel. It's a bunch of words on paper. He didn't actually do this to a woman. It's a sentence he wrote where that happens, not a real woman he chained by her neck.

What else could I say? The novel was what it was. The students could accept that or drop out of school. Neither action would change the contents of the novel.

The novel was what the novel was, the class was the class it was, and I was the professor they were stuck with. The other ones weren't that different. We all had guns.

It had changed things, our having the guns.

I didn't think about it when I was alone with my gun. I didn't notice it then. I noticed it when we were out together, two or more of us professors, getting coffee or getting lunch. People gave us a wide berth. They showed us a spatial respect I hadn't been shown before, when I was one of the unarmed faculty.

I don't know how the civilians knew who we were, when we went out together. We didn't wear uniforms. It was as if everyone could feel, primally, that we were different, that we were either potentially dangerous or potentially their protectors. The air around us had a static charge I've only ever associated with police.

It was the guns that made this happen. I thought so, anyway. Like cops, we had instruments of death strapped to our bodies; people we came across seemed to feel it just under their skin and react accordingly.

It could be that Shirley was right, that the guns had changed our behaviors, made us more attuned to the vibrations in the air that would tell us if danger was near, like spiders who feel for vibrations on their webs. The guns had most likely changed the way we stood, the way we walked, the ways we assessed the threat potential of strangers.

Daniel said, when I talked about it with him, that he enjoyed this effect his gun had on other people. For him, it was one of the perks of the job. Daniel had, of course, always carried a gun. Before, it wasn't because he was a teacher. It was because he was Daniel. But since Teach and Carry passed, and wearing a gun was part of his job, he was given a certain respect that meant an awful lot to him.

I had to admit, when he told me that, that before we had guns I'd found that the respect I was supposed to get as a professor eluded me. Before I became a professor, I would hear about the status that was conferred on professors. People always used that word, when discussing it: status. They said it made up for the low salaries. All the status did.

What status? I'd say to Shirley. What respect? The students don't respect me. I don't get good seats at restaurants because I'm an English professor. No one listens to most of what I say.

Shirley would shrug. She didn't seem to care very much about my lack of status.

This new respect I was getting, with the gun—or the fear I was inspiring, more likely—didn't come only from people at delis and bakeries. It came from politicians, and other such people. Teachers, now, were listed among the groups that had their support.

Before Teach and Carry, we'd been openly vilified—unions broken, layoffs celebrated—as if our jobs did not involve helping people, making them smarter and making their lives better. As if we hadn't chosen to make low salaries because it meant something to us to do something meaningful, something for the greater good. The United States had always seemed to look on its teachers as an enormous population of lay-about distant cousins, living liabilities to the sensible and business-minded world. We were bad examples to the children, they seemed to think, and should have all gone to school for business and opened a business.

That attitude changed, when we got our guns. Everything changed, except how much students didn't like the things I assigned to them to read. They kept not liking any of that.

Everything had changed thanks to the bloodbath in Anchorage, the coordinated attack on Alaska's flagship university by two men who weren't even enrolled there. They killed students; they killed teachers. More people died than in any other school shooting, which was saying something. The killers melted into the woods beside a highway, and weren't caught, and so could only be assumed

175

to be out there still, who knew where, with bandanas to pin across their faces and assault rifles locked and loaded.

They could reemerge from those words, or any other woods, any time they wanted, and so colleges had to be on constant yellow alert. Even if the Anchorage guys didn't come to another campus with murder on their minds, someone else would. It happened all the time, a dozen times a year, now, at least.

You have to arm the teachers, said the House, the Senate, and executive branch, which is all you need to pass a law. It says so in the Constitution, the same one the second amendment is in.

When we finally got around to talking about the novel we'd started, *All the Pretty Horses*, things had taken a turn. The students had been impatient with *Blood Meridian*. Now, toward the first installment of the *Border Trilogy*, they were borderline hostile.

What in the world is this book, said Gary.

Right? agreed Riley the girl. What is this guy's deal?

What do you mean? I said.

The horses, said Pygmalion. I get it. He likes horses.

You can like horses all you want, said Addison. That doesn't mean you get to write weird paragraphs about them.

Why not?

Because it's boring.

Phillip sat with his arms folded. He was glaring at me.

You can think this book is boring, I said. You can think that. But there is real substance here.

I have wanted to get across, but haven't known when or how to do it, that Phillip was black. He was the only black student in the class, and it doesn't matter, except that I want to mention it, and it sort of does matter. How can I convey, without breaking what continuity there is here, that Phillip was African American? I don't want to refer directly to the color of his skin; that wouldn't be right. He didn't do anything particularly blackly, whatever that would mean; there is no moment in my time spent with him I can pinpoint, or characteristic behavior he exhibited, that, if I mentioned it, or described it, would communicate Phillip's racial identity. He was black. It's worth getting that across, if only because if I don't then everyone will assume he was white. They will picture him as someone other than Phillip.

I have wondered if this is something Cormac McCarthy ever wrestled with, too, perhaps when he was writing *Outer Dark*, where if you take one character and read him as non-white—whoever it is—then the equation of the novel is altered considerably. I have wondered if there are characters in his novels who are meant to be understood not to be white, but who we assume are white nevertheless. Maybe the protagonist of *Blood Meridian* is black. I don't think it ever says that he isn't.

I didn't mention this in my lecture on *All the Pretty Horses*. Instead I talked about loss and companionship, about a dynamic that recurred throughout McCarthy's work: two men walk along a road on their way someplace, not sure exactly where they're going. It happens in his novels, I said, over and over.

I un-squinted my eyes, at one point, and surveyed the class. I gauged their interest.

They weren't interested.

I was going to have to do something to reel them in.

The class hadn't been like this all along—not quite. The first novel we'd read was *Outer Dark*. We'd skipped *The Orchard Keeper* because it is a garbage novel that no one should have to read. They were okay with *Outer Dark*, right up until the first infant death of the semester, which was at the very end of *Outer Dark*.

This is horrible, said Riley the boy, when we reached that point.

I almost threw up when I read that, said Bella.

I believed her. She seemed like someone who would almost throw up.

Probably the most disgusted of them all was Addison, with her blonde eyebrows and jet-black hair who had been more than eager, ever since we began discussing *Outer Dark*, to volunteer her distaste for what we were reading.

Addison's primary reason for not liking *Outer Dark*, she said, was that it was unrealistic. I don't think, she said, that anyone in anyplace would have a real life like this. Would get pregnant and then just wander off without the baby. What kind of mother would do that? How can any mother not love her child?

She had a point, sort of. I said so. I tried telling her that this behavior was not outside the realm of possibility, though, and wondered as I spoke if her reaction was an indication of something that might have happened in her life. Maybe she had abandoned a child in the woods and wandered away from it. Maybe she had been the abandoned child.

I looked her up on Twitter that night and found no evidence there of child abandonment. I did find a tweet that read,

I cant [sic] believe I have to read this novel

It was punctuated with an emoticon it is beyond my powers to reproduce. It seemed to denote a mixture of confusion, anger, consternation and physical pain.

Throughout our conversations about *Outer Dark*, I tried to elevate our discussions and transcend gut-level reactions like horror and disbelief. I wanted to talk about the hangings—or lynchings—that the characters see evidence of, and which they identify as inevitable aspects of the world they inhabit. It must, I wanted to say, indicate that McCarthy was mindful as he wrote of the lynchings that plagued the South at the time. The book was published in 1968, after all.

In *Outer Dark*, I remember telling my class, we have two characters who are traversing a hazardous and unforgiving landscape. One of them has been wronged, the other has attempted to murder a newborn. You have the wronger and the wronged, both lost on the same road.

I don't like that I said the word "wronger"—it makes me sound like I don't know enough words—but the point was that in *Outer Dark* McCarthy has boiled down all the moral shortcomings of the South in the 1960s and presented it to us in as simplified a form as possible. And of course that's no substitute for a real understanding of the South; you can't read *Outer Dark* and think you know much about a real time and place. But McCarthy isn't interested in the realities of the South; he doesn't care about *what really happened*. His novel is more like the silhouette of a real time and place than an attempt to render that time and place.

It's an experiment. And a daring one—one that's bound to be alienating to some people. Like, for example, all nine of my students.

One thing I could say for my nine students was that they were honest. I value that, to an extent.

They were honest about how much they hated *All the Pretty Horses*. When we reached our final discussion of it, their gloves came off, because they didn't like the way it ended.

Of course they didn't. They didn't like anything that led up to the end, so why would they approve of the ending?

I don't like the part about the reverend, said Addison. The radio guy, I mean. The preacher on the radio.

I knew who she meant.

He's irrelevant, said Riley the boy. He had nothing to do with the rest of the novel.

I was at a point that I didn't even want to tell Riley the boy he didn't know what he was talking about, that the reverend had everything to do with the rest of the novel. He talks casually, and disdainfully, about the Russians of the world, when it's clear that he hasn't done what the protagonist has spent the novel doing: crossing a border and encountering people on its other side, sometimes with terrible consequences, and well outside the safety of a radio booth. The preacher can reach people with his technology without exposing himself to reprisal, without being harmed. The protagonist enjoys no such luxury. He suffers.

I suffered, too, every minute I spent in the classroom with those students.

Whereas, if I taught classes online, I wouldn't have had to hear their bad ideas in person; they'd have been abstracted by the technology that mitigated our contact with one another.

Nor would I have feared the gunman like I did; he wouldn't have known where my house was, probably, and he wouldn't have wanted to kill me because he would not have met me. If he were like other schoolhouse killers, he wouldn't come for me, because I lived alone, and staging a shooting at my house would yield a low body count.

What an American obsession that is, Shirley said once: the obsession on the part of our suicidal killers with having the highest body count of anyone. Like baseball scouts, they study the techniques of prior killers. They draw up spreadsheets. They're as meticulous about planning massacres as pitchers are about perfecting their curveballs. They want to be the best psychos in history, like each one has a chance at getting his face on a Wheaties box in Hell if he surpasses his psychotic forebears.

I sat in my office, after the last class session we spent talking about *All the Pretty Horses* and came closer to quitting my chosen profession altogether than I had ever come.

This was it. I couldn't do it anymore. I had to give up or change my approach. I had my gun on my desk, and I was spinning it around, like a game of Spin the Bottle but with a gun and no one to kiss.

After fifteen minutes of Spin the Gun on the Table, I had a plan, which I spent the next day setting in motion.

The next time we met, we were starting our penultimate text, *No Country for Old Men*. We were skipping *The Crossing* and *Cities of the Plain* because I'd never read the latter and we didn't have time for the former. We had to skip a couple of the novels, and I thought we might as well skip the one where a wolf dies when it's full of unborn wolves, plus the next one.

We were gathered in class to begin our weeks-long conversation on the novel—I, that is, and the six students who bothered to show up that day. But before we dove into the novel, I had something special to show them.

I didn't call it that. The best way to ensure that students of the current generation of students turn against you is to refer to something as "special." They don't go for words like that.

I downplayed it. I said I wanted to show them just a thing I had. I said it was basically nothing.

We haven't spent much time this semester, I said, talking about writing process. Not McCarthy's writing process, anyway. We don't discuss that generally—how a book or anything else gets written. We treat these things like things that weren't written *by* someone but that coalesced on their own, without authors making them.

Well, that's how this field works, right? The author's dead, even when he's not. We can't change that. But for today, we're going to break that rule.

So, all right, I said. When McCarthy writes, he uses the same machine, an Olivetti Lettera 32. It's a manual typewriter, not an electric one. They're usually green. They were made in Spain.

Why does that matter? Well, what I want to show you is something that was typed on his typewriter. Because he wrote it.

This is something I haven't mentioned, I said, because I haven't wanted to be accused of nepotism, or anything. But I actually know Cormac McCarthy. I know him personally.

I don't know him *that* well. I wouldn't say we're best friends. But some years back I was presenting at his annual conference, and someone who knows him better than I do liked what I was saying, and we were introduced, via correspondence. He writes *real* letters, on paper, the old-fashioned way.

It's gotten to where I'm one of the people he'll send something new when it's making its way to publication. There are actually a bunch of us, but not that many.

It's not for feedback purposes. He's just generating buzz. Not that he calls it that. I think his publisher puts him up to it. But anyway, I'm not really supposed to do this, but I'm going to do it.

That got the students' attention. Maybe they were scared, because the man who was saying he would now do something he shouldn't had a gun on his person. Among the things I wasn't supposed to do, and could have done, was shoot the students. Or myself.

I don't think that was why they stirred to attention, though. I think they thought I was going to do something wrong, something dumb. This generation of young people want nothing more than to see someone self-destruct in public. They want to film it and put it online. I said, I'm not supposed to share these pages with you, because they were given to me in confidence. But I've copied them, and I want you to see them, since by now you're all basically experts on the guy.

Which, of course, they weren't. Most of them had read next to nothing all semester and would fail the course if I could afford to fail them, if the administration didn't frown on it so. They were desperate to retain students, even the worst of them.

The students in my World Literature class may have been the worst students in the whole college. Probably not. But, bad students or not, I had to regain their confidence.

I wasn't willing to do what Daniel had suggested: consider this a learning experience, accept failure and move on. I wanted to be a good professor. I wanted them to like me and say so in my evaluations.

I didn't want to be a professor only for the job title and the low salary and general disregard I got from most people. I wanted to be, if not an effective teacher, one that the students thought was *with it*—if not smart, then connected to something bigger than myself and considered valuable.

Together we read the pages I'd distributed. Phillip volunteered to read them aloud.

When he was done, I explained why the pages looked the way they did. They don't, I said, look anything like the kind of printed-out stuff we're used to. Do they? They were written on McCarthy's typewriter, then photocopied, probably by his assistant, if he has one. He probably has one.

Of course the two pages I'd distributed were written by me. They were typed not on McCarthy's Olivetti Lettera 32, but on the one I had acquired a couple of years prior, when

I learned that it was what McCarthy used. I hadn't been planning, then, to undertake this minor subterfuge. I hadn't thought things would come to this.

I'll admit, though, that I had some fun writing the pages on the manual typewriter. I'll admit that I have some affection for things that are made of metal and aren't electric. There I was, a couple of nights in a row, late at night, trying to sit the way I thought McCarthy might sit, on my couch, hammering the keys.

The typewriter is a lovely machine, one that does exactly what it's meant to do. My Olivetti Lettera 32 is more than fifty years old and it serves its purpose wonderfully, that purpose being forging manuscript pages by famous authors. No planned obsolescence there. No, sir.

A couple of pages into writing the fake stuff, I wondered if, in fact, the cure for gun enthusiasm lay in the revival of metal devices that don't use electricity. It's not such a wild idea.

The things I like about the typewriter are the same things I like about my gun. They look handsome in their own ways; they're wonderfully efficient. When I press down on a typewriter key and when I pull the pistol's trigger, something happens, and you can feel and hear it happen. Both things that happen are loud and make strong impressions, different as those impressions are, and vastly different as their immediate consequences can be. Maybe, I found myself wondering, the reason why we have gun nuts is that guns are some of the only things whose purposes haven't been subsumed by newer, flashier, plastic devices. All those handsome film cameras of the 50s and 60s were made obsolete by phones. Plastic electronic phones do all the things that metal things once did that had moving parts and no batteries. Maybe one reason people fall in love with guns is that they're some of the only simple machines left in the world.

How, then, could we deter people from growing fascinated by guns and buying them, and starting them down the path to murder-suicide?

I think one part of the cure for our nation's gun frenzy is the return of analog metal objects, like clocks and watches that have moving parts. We could have fewer computers of all shapes and sizes. We could give the gun nuts different things to spend their baffling disposable incomes on—things that have some of the appealing features that guns have, but without the lethal functionality. Let them have typewriters. Let them have telescopes and stethoscopes. See if they can't get their rocks off with those.

The fake Cormac McCarthy thing I wrote was one short scene that was meant to have come from his next novel, *Nightstalker*.

There is no way he would write a novel called that, but the students were unlikely to be moved to care enough to infer that, from the titles of the books they'd mostly declined to read in months past.

What happens in the scene from *Nightstalker* is that the protagonist, James Nightstalker, enters an open field where there is also a wild horse.

He stood in the field and watched the horse at the far end of the clearing,

I had written the night before, while drinking.

The horse drank from the stream that ran there and Nightstalker drank from his canteen and watched the horse drink. He watched the horse and the horse watched the clearing.

This goes on for a while. When you're imitating Cormac McCarthy's prose style, it's easy to get carried away with the sentences. I don't know how he makes anything happen

in them, the sentences are so prone to lying down like—
what the hell—like stubborn horses and refusing to move.
But he makes them move.

Eventually, another man appears in the clearing, and
The two men regarded one another with the cold bearing
down on their skin and on the horse that stood still in the
clearing. The man approached Nightstalker greeting him
with himself and his voice. He lit a cigarette and stopped to
do it. He stepped forward. Nightstalker watched him come.

Nightstalker ends up murdering the guy. I had to write a
murder into the scene. This one involved a knife.

Nightstalker's hand gripped the knife. The man pleaded
and fell to his knees.

No, he said. Please, no.

Nightstalker thrust the knife and met flesh. The man who
was not

Nightstalker gasped and could plead no more as he
watched his blood spill redly onto the grass.

Across the clearing the horse watched and continued to
watch.

It ended there, because I didn't want to spend too much
time in class on this fake writing. Plus I didn't know where
else the scene should go, after the abrupt murder that made
no sense.

Why was the horse there? I didn't know. I trusted the
students to assume that the missing context would supply
that information in the complete novel.

I collected the photocopies from the students, telling
them it was imperative that I get them all, for if one fell into
the wrong hands it could jeopardize my role as a McCarthy
scholar and occasional confidante.

I didn't mean to give them ideas.

We talked for a little while about the Nightstalker pages.
They had questions about them. Addison asked what the

envelope was like that they came in. I made something up about it being plain brown. Phillip asked what the whole novel was about, since it wasn't clear from those two pages. I was tempted to say it was about a guy who for his whole life is followed by a horse, even when he goes to other countries. I didn't say that.

I told them the truth: I said I wasn't sure. Then I lied and said there had been talk on a listserv about the novel being about Nightstalker's search for his father's grave. Phillip nodded, with his hand on his chin, like he was really thinking about that. Riley the girl asked what I myself thought of the pages.

It was a tough question. Ooh, I said. Well, I smiled. Honestly? It's not his best. It's not great.

Don't writers, asked Riley the boy, get worse as they age?

Huh, I said. I don't think so.

Doesn't this sample from the next novel suggest that?

Not necessarily. I don't know. This could be just a dud. It might make more sense, in context.

Didn't you say, asked Riley the girl, that the last couple of books by this guy weren't good?

I did say that. Sort of. But you can't judge a whole book by a two-page sample. And they're not *that* bad.

They're pretty bad, said Pygmalion.

You think so?

I think so, said Phillip. What's with the standing horse? All it does is stand. He keeps mentioning it, but it doesn't do anything. I don't care about the horse. And he stabs the other guy for no reason.

It's dumb, said Riley the boy.

And bad, said Riley the girl.

Well, I said. I really do think the pages leave out a certain amount of context, which is necessary to knowing what's going on.

By the time I'd said that, I'd lost them. We had run out of time, anyway.

The pages leaked, three weeks later.

I didn't know which of the bastards did it. I was sure I had collected all of the copies I'd distributed to them in good faith. I was wrong, apparently, because there, on an anonymously created Tumblr page, were the pages I'd distributed to the students. It described them just as I had, as a scene from Cormac McCarthy's to-be-released next novel, *Nightstalker*, the first installment in the *Horse Book Trilogy*. I had called it that in class, not dreaming it would end up online.

There was no indication I could see online that the pages had come from my typewriter. Whatever student had posted them had spared me the humiliation of saying I was their source. It seemed that he, or she, may not have put it together that I'd written the pages. The culprit may have thought he really was leaking pages from a McCarthy novel, rather than outing me as a fraud.

It wasn't clear. There wasn't much text to accompany the fake McCarthy excerpt, which made sense. To write more than a short paragraph about anything was not something my students excelled at, and the things they wrote in their papers were not exactly well-shaped paragraphs.

The accompanying statement was standard internet stuff. It said, You won't believe this! Pages from the next McCarthy revealed!

I don't know how the word spread, given the inanity of that statement; or, I didn't know at first how it spread, until I looked and saw that whatever student of mine posted it, under the Tumblr alias GrapeBoy666, had several thousand followers and a Tumblr history that must have meant that Tumblr for him, or her, was a full-time job. If every student had something like this going on, it might help explain why they were such bad, distracted students.

The pages were seen by a lot of people, I don't know how many. I don't know how I would have found out how many. I only found out the pages were on Tumblr because my colleagues at other institutions posted links to them and pointed out on Facebook how absurd they were. It was through Facebook that I learned that the student who'd posted the pages said his teacher had given them to him, and said they were authentic.

I thought the best way to prevent the pages from getting traced back to me was to participate in the discussion, so on my Facebook page I posted a link to the pages and talked there about what an injustice it was that those poor students were not being taken more seriously, that the college— wherever it was—was being disrespected in this way.

Colleagues from other schools had fun with that statement. They commented on my post that the students wouldn't know they were being disrespected unless someone tweeted at them about it, or posted the news on Tumblr—which, I didn't point out, was more or less what had actually happened.

I did think, though, that I should bring recent developments to attention of the students. I shared with them the Tumblr page in class, but I didn't let on that I thought any of them had created it. I told them the Tumblr page must have been created by a student at another school, where another professor had also shared the pages with his students. I said I should have known they were fake. I apologized to them for not vetting the pages properly. I pretended I had been fooled right along with them.

The students were as stone-faced as always, as I talked and scanned the room to see if someone would flinch, or break out in a grin, to let on that he or she was the one who had leaked the pages. I caught no such sign. I kept looking out for signs in our class sessions that followed, but there weren't many sessions left.

It was all very bad. But it wasn't the worst thing I did that semester, not the only thing I did in the name of trying to make the students think I was better, smarter and more important than I was.

Before the pages made their way onto Tumblr, but after I'd shown them to the students, I took one extra measure to convince the class of my greatness.

Why did I want them to think I was great? I don't know. It's one of those things that's hard to be certain about, let alone explain.

I certainly wasn't doing things anymore to help the students learn. I wasn't defrauding them in the name of their increased knowledge of world literature.

I suppose I understood in my blood and bones, with the gun against my chest, that schools weren't places to learn things anymore. Not like they once were.

Before I was a gun-toting professor, I would never have wanted to make the students think I was the Monster Mind, the most preeminent man in my field, or whatever. I had always gotten by on the simple baseline respect that one needs to have in order for the classroom to function. Most students handed this over to professors readily. As long as no one's calling me an asshole in class, I can teach just fine.

I had gone far beyond that, now, and demanded more from the students, not so much in the way of classroom performance, but definitely in the way of adulation.

It must have been partly due to the way these kids were so checked out. They could only be moved to care about their work if it meant not liking something I'd asked them to read. Their indifference only fanned the flames of my need for them to think I was brilliant. It only worsened my need for their approval.

The gun must have had something to do with it. Not that I mean to suggest I had a psychic connection with it now, or that it came to life and whispered my inadequacy in my ear at night when I slept, so that I woke up every day needing more affirmation from the people around me than the day before, and so on.

Shirley was right when she said, before we parted for good, that with the gun I was different than I'd been without it, that it brought on a personality change. I understand that better, now that I'm outside of teaching, in the aftermath of my teaching life. Looking back, it seems to me that there were lots of things I did when I had my gun that I wouldn't have done before the gun. The gun had changed things.

There was Amy, for example, whom I only spoke with once. She came to my office during office hours, late one afternoon, as I sat at my desk cleaning my gun. I was just reinserting the firing pin when there was a knock at the door. I looked up to see a demure young woman (Amy) with blonde hair in a sweater and plaid skirt. She had half a smile on her face. No one had ever seen me cleaning my gun before, not even Shirley.

Are you Professor Johnson? asked Amy.

I put my disassembled gun down. Yes, I said. I mean, no. What do you want him for?

I didn't mean for it to sound confrontational. It did, though.

Amy didn't say what she wanted Professor Johnson for. Can you tell me where his office is? she said. She wasn't half-smiling anymore.

It was down the hall, I said. You mean Chad Johnson, right?

I think so, she said. She looked at the paper in her hand. Yes, she said.

Chad hasn't taught here in four years, I said. I think it's four years. Why did you want him?

She looked confused. She stood looking down at the paper, and I wondered if she was trying to decide how soon she should leave.

She didn't leave. I'm trying to sign up for classes, she said. I wanted to take one of his. The British Novel?

Right. 309.

Yes.

I teach that, now.

The course bulletin says Johnson teaches it. Why does it say that?

I'm not sure. A lot of people who don't teach here still show up on the course bulletins. I think it's an accreditation thing.

It wasn't really an accreditation thing. I don't know what it was, I was just saying things.

Do you want, I said, to talk to me about the class?

Amy looked up at me. She'd been looking at the course bulletin in her hand. She seemed like one of those people you meet sometimes, who would rather stand there staring at a course bulletin than look another person in the face. Okay, she said. She sat in the extra chair, and I swept my gun parts aside. She sat poised as if ready to leave quickly, if necessary.

Maybe she was ready to leave quickly, if necessary. She didn't know for sure that I didn't have another gun, maybe in a desk drawer. For all she knew, I didn't even really teach there.

She didn't seem suspicious. She seemed reticent, but so do most students. She told me she had wanted to speak to Johnson about his job generally. She was not an English major, but was thinking of becoming one, as it had always been a secret dream of hers to become an English professor. Johnson had taught in the field that interested her most. I love Oscar Wilde, she said.

I didn't have the heart to tell her—I never do—that loving a thing is not a reason to study it and be a professor of it. In fact, if anything, it's a reason not to do that. It's a disadvantage. Or maybe I am jaded.

So you're teaching his class, she said, even though it's not your field?

That question threw me. Most students don't know that professors have fields. They know we have guns. Specializations are more of a mystery to the average student. Amy was a little older than the average student; she looked about 23. Sometimes that makes all the difference.

It's not my primary field, I said. But we're all generalists now, more or less. We have to be versatile. What do you find so attractive about 19C?

I said it like that, *19C*. I don't know why. Professors don't talk like that. She just said again that she really liked Oscar Wilde. She said she believed that everyone should have access to a good education. The humanities matter to me, she said. I think they're just as important as science.

Well, I said. You know, if you'd come to talk with me about this (she hadn't come to talk with *me* about it at all) eight years ago, I would have said, forget it. There's no way you'll find a job doing this.

Really.

Yeah. There were too many people getting PhDs. Not enough jobs. Now, though, it's hard to find people to take the jobs.

Why is that?

They don't pay well.

Oh.

And the gun thing.

Right.

There are adjuncts. Part-time faculty, I mean.

They don't want to be full-time?

No, they do.

But you don't make them full-time.

I made a face. Them? I said.

I guess? It would make sense to me.

It's not happening, I said. But probably the main thing that keeps people from wanting to teach at colleges is all the shootings.

There aren't that many shootings.

I grinned. Finally, someone understood. I know, I said. There really aren't. And a lot of gunmen are getting stopped. And not even by the person teaching the class that's under attack. I don't have the stats memorized, but they looked good when I saw them last.

Is that the gun you use? said Amy.

What, this? Yeah. Usually in one piece, though.

Do you think five bullets are enough?

What?

The Ruger SP101. It's only got five chambers.

Okay.

If someone attacks your students, you could miss five times. What if the gunman doesn't let you reload?

Amy was smiling again, in a way that made me wonder for a second if Daniel hadn't sent her as a kind of prank.

I'm a very good shot, I said.

Okay, she said, nodding, still smiling.

It wasn't like she didn't have a point. But I didn't need to hear this from Amy.

I changed the subject. We talked about grad schools. She said she didn't want to leave the region for grad school, which limited her options, but I gave her a short list of schools to consider. Tennyson College, I said, is one to look at, maybe visit. I said I heard they had an actual minefield in place that only the students and faculty knew about.

What about the staff?

Right, I said. They probably told the staff it was there.

Not the adjuncts, though, right?

Yeah, I laughed. Not if they've got any sense.

The entire time I spoke with Amy she seemed somehow like only half of her was sitting in my office, like the other half of her was already in the future. It was a bright future, brighter than mine.

I surmised that Amy was blessed with greater intelligence and ability and ambition than most people, with a good work ethic to boot. I am sensitive to this sort of thing. When I talk to someone like Amy, I can feel myself being left behind, left out of a better life than the one I'm in. I could see it already: I had known Amy for only fifteen minutes, but I knew she would go someplace nearby for her graduate work, where as a teaching associate she would become an expert markswoman, and she would return to teach in my department. In her first year she would get both a teaching award and a shooting award. I didn't think all of this in so many words; it was just a feeling I had, and a bad one, which stuck with me, and helped lead me to the next questionable pedagogical strategy I took that semester.

It's not that I didn't see that I'd already taken a great risk, when lying to my students the first time. As soon as I saw the *Nightstalker* excerpt, linked via the Facebook pages of my friends at other institutions, I knew that if I were found out it would mean the end of my Cormac McCarthy class, my membership to the McCarthy Society—which is mistaken sometimes for the Mary McCarthy Society, which doesn't exist—and probably my teaching career.

It was probably worse than writing a fake McCarthy excerpt and giving it to students, as far as ethics go.

I brought the students another surprise.

You are not going to believe this, I said, until you see it. I got Cormac McCarthy, I said, to do a Skype interview with this class.

You did what? asked Weird Al, who almost never came to class, and whom only I called Weird Al, in my head. Everyone else just called him Al.

No way, said Phillip.

Yes, I said. I didn't think I could do it, but I wrote Cormac a letter, and asked if it was possible. And it is possible.

It wasn't possible. Of course it wasn't. I had hired an actor named Craig, who looked like Cormac McCarthy and had a Skype account, to pretend to be Cormac McCarthy.

He really did look like Cormac McCarthy. His actor webpage listed the people he resembled: Bob Newhart, Bob Hope, and Cormac McCarthy.

He didn't look anything like either of the Bobs. When I read their names on his celebrity resemblance list, I wondered if he should see an eye doctor.

He did look an awful lot like McCarthy, though, which was the only thing I cared about, for the purposes of the Skype call. McCarthy appeared on the back covers of all the students' books, and they would know an impostor if they saw one. Their eyes were fine.

Craig lived in California, so there was no chance the students would recognize him as Craig or see him in public later and mistake him for Cormac McCarthy. Plus he was a loser; the students wouldn't see him and recognize him from any movies or TV shows, because he hadn't been in any of either thing. He hadn't even done commercials.

He sounded smart enough on the phone. I asked for his best vaguely Appalachian/western accent, and it sounded convincing. Craig said he had read all of McCarthy's novels—not for my sake, but because he often made appearances as the famous author.

You do? I said.

Yes, he said.

Like where?

Academic conferences. Not the good ones.

Really?

Yeah. They don't let me say anything. They just ask me to walk in and stand in the back during a presentation and look stern until they're done. Then I leave, before anyone can try to talk to me.

Who does?

Who does what?

Who hires you to do that?

Oh. The guy presenting. Or the gal. There are never a lot of people there, so when I come in, they know who I'm supposed to be, and they get all hot and bothered and eager to talk to me when it's over. But by then I'm already gone. It's supposed to seem like I'm interested in the guy who's talking, the guy who hired me, but only him. I guess it's a tenure thing?

It wasn't a tenure thing. That's not the sort of thing that will get you tenure. It was a respect thing. It was something you would do if you wanted your peers to respect you more, and it was brilliant. I wished I had thought of it.

But then, the conferences I go to are the ones where attendees would know the difference between Cormac McCarthy and Craig.

I think they would, anyway.

I don't want to dwell on the Craig episode, as it's not my proudest episode. If I were proud of it, I wouldn't call it an episode.

I didn't want to give Craig too much time to talk with the students, because the longer he talked the more likely they were to figure out what a lie I had told them. I had him Skype us during the last twenty minutes of our class, the prior thirty minutes of which I spent telling them what was wrong with *No Country for Old Men* and why it didn't live up to the rest of McCarthy's oeuvre.

I could tell by the looks on the students' faces that they didn't know what an oeuvre was. I paraphrased the Coen brothers, who said on Charlie Rose once that *No Country for Old Men* was a pulpier novel than what McCarthy usually wrote, which is a polite way of saying it isn't very good.

When Craig's face appeared on the big screen at the front of the room, I had to admit he was convincing. He looked nothing at all like Bob Newhart, but it was as if Cormac McCarthy himself were looking down on us with a giant face on a screen—something like Big Brother, or Max Headroom.

I exchanged pleasantries with Craig on behalf of the class, calling him Mack, as planned, so that the students would think he and I were really friends.

I just want to tell you, first of all, he said, how happy I am to be here today. As you know I am one of those writers who hides. I keep my head down and all things considered I would rather be with scientists than other writers. Why? (no one had asked this; he was just talking) I guess it's not clear. I guess you could say that as a writer I feel more like a scientist than an artist of the regular kind.

It's not an arrogance thing. I'm not above anyone. It has to do with the way I approach things, the way I get words down. It's not one word after another and then more words and another one. I don't do that and then go back and see what themes I've created in rewrites.

I am a much more careful man than that. More calculated. More precise. Like a Hunter.

Like Hunter S. Thompson? asked Weird Al.

What? said Craig. No. Like a real hunter. With that kind of precision. Precision is what makes a man a writer. I believe that and I believe you can see that in Anton Chigurh, a character I created, whose name I came up with because I thought it was interesting.

I thought he would stop talking, but he didn't stop talking.

Now, he said, you probably know I don't make many appearances. I am not a man who gets seen by just anybody. I don't go places for money or for any other reason—unless that reason is that a friend is in need. That is something I will honor, because I am a southern gentleman. I will honor the need of a dear friend like my friend here.

I understand you know him as Professor. That's not how I know him. I am proud to say that with all my heart.

Oh, come on, now, Mack, I said. You're embarrassing me.

And he was, but not in the way that the students were meant to understand it.

Craig said, I understand you all have questions you wanted to ask. I made it clear to my friend here, my dear friend, that I would answer your questions as long as you do not publish the answers, as long as they do not leave this conversation.

That's right, I said. They understand.

All right, then. Ask away.

The first question came from Pygmalion. She read the question from the notecard she held in her hand.

Mr. McCarthy, she said.

Please, he interrupted. Call me Mack.

Okay, Mack. Where do you get your inspiration from?

That's a question, he said. That is a question. You have asked a question, young lady. I suppose the best way I can answer it is to go back to a novel I wrote a while back that finally put a feather in my cap that we writers call the Pulitzer Prize.

That book is *The Road*. It is the one about the end of the world, and its inspiration came from a special place in my mind and my heart.

I was with my son, and we were on vacation. I don't recall, to be honest, the specific place, but I was there in a hotel and we heard this lonely whistle. It was a whistle that came across the plain, and I don't know what it was or what made it. I had a vision of a man and his boy alone in a vast emptiness and fighting to survive. And somewhere in there a baby getting killed.

Do you get that vision a lot? asked Addison.

Sure, said Craig.

I wasn't sure how well he'd heard what Addison said.

And then, said Craig, the cannibals came into it later. I thought they'd be a good way to provide a reason for the baby dying.

The explanation Craig was giving Addison for where *The Road* came from, is more or less what McCarthy told Oprah about where *The Road* came from. Craig had told me in an email that he'd committed to memory the contents of McCarthy's appearance on *Oprah*. So he'd really said something like that, about the whistle, or whatever.

But then, if you look at other novels he wrote prior to *The Road*, you see elements that also appear in *The Road*, things that that novel repeats, which clearly didn't come out of his vacation with his son—which must have been a good time, by the way. Take *Outer Dark*, once again, which follows a brother and sister as they traverse a nightmare landscape on separate paths. There are people being hanged for no apparent reason, and it's treated in their passing conversations as an inevitable turn of events, the direction the world was going in all along. *Outer Dark* is like a prequel to *The Road*, the way *Mad Max* is a prequel to *Mad Max 2*; things are clearly going wrong, in the first one, but in a general, nonspecific way. And then in the second movie the whole world has turned to Hell.

About that, said Phillip. Your novels have a lot of babies getting killed in them. And mutilated.

Yes, said Craig with enthusiasm.

Two at a time, sometimes, said Phillip.

Indeed, young man. Indeed. I can sense in your tone some consternation. Perhaps condemnation. And I assure you, you are not the first to condemn me and my work.

I don't want you to get the false impression that I am some kind of freak. Or that I write such imagery lightly. Or that I don't understand that putting such things into the world, getting that stuff into other people's heads, is not its own form of violence. When I write the death of a fictional child, I do it with caution. In fact, in order to ensure that I understand the gravity of it all, when I write those scenes, I picture my own son, as a baby, dying in place of the one that I made up.

Huh, said Weird Al. Really?

That's right.

So, when you're writing, you like to picture your son's head exploding, or getting cooked and eaten?

Yes, said Craig, uncertainly, nodding. But for the right reasons, he said. It's for art.

Maybe I should ask the next question, I said.

Shoot, said Craig, using a word lightly that shouldn't be used lightly in a classroom, even by someone who is Skyping.

Something that's been on my mind this semester as we've read *Pretty Horses* are the many flourishes you included in the novel.

Yes. The flourishes.

You know what I mean, then?

About the horses' eyelids and things.

That's right. That's what I mean. Where the horses kind of start a sentence and then run off with it into the field and the dust and the mud of creation that poured over the earth and settled there to make the dirt that grew to be horses.

Okay.

That kind of stuff.

I will tell you about those flourishes. I did not intend for them to become what they became. Not at first. I feel like what they turned into after a long while are paragraphs that flow the way a horse runs. They start with a trot that becomes a gambol and they break into a run. But the way that started out was, I was having some writer's block, and I would write the first part of a sentence, and then get up and move, you know, like go out for a walk or a ride, on Buckeye, my horse. And I'd come back and pick up where I left off. I wouldn't look at what I wrote before, I would just keep going. And this would go on for days. And when I was done, I'd have these big, long paragraphs about horses. All right, I said to myself. I'll keep these. I'll call them flourishes.

That's a great story.

Isn't it? Sometimes great literature is a happy accident. I've always believed that.

You have? asked Phillip.

Of course, young man. Indeed, I have. Indeed.

Bella was the next deadbeat to ask a question. What, she said, about the women in your novels?

There was a silence, and for a moment I thought we might have lost Mack to buffering. But he was only being very still and silent, until he said, Is there more to the question?

No.

What about the women? said Craig. That's what you're asking me?

Yes.

Okay. Well. Which women do you have in mind? There aren't many.

That's why I'm asking, said Bella.

It is?

I mean, she said, when there are women in your novels it means something bad is happening.

Bad how?

Like to the men. For the men in your novels, women are problems.

I don't know about that.

You don't? What about the mother in *All the Pretty Horses*? She betrays her son and sells the ranch. And then he falls for a woman south of the border, who almost gets him killed.

Okay, said Craig. All right.

Then in *The Road*, Bella said—revealing she had read ahead—the wife gets one chance to talk in the whole book, and it's all because she's dead, I know, that she's not around to talk. She can only appear in a flashback, which is convenient. But the thing is, when she does talk, she's just this raving harpy cunt.

Woah, young lady, said Craig. That's your word. I didn't say that.

She's so cruel to the dad, and not in a way that women really are. Women definitely wouldn't be that bad after the world ended. It's so unnecessary.

Bella was done talking, now. She could see she'd made her point. Craig was looking away, now. He was uncertain what to do. I hadn't prepared him for this.

I don't think Bella even wanted a response. Not really. I think she just wanted to speak truth to Cormac McCarthy.

The joke was on her.

What Craig did say, ultimately, was probably a thing he shouldn't have said, which was that while women in real life weren't often as bad as his women were there are some bad apples out there. That was how he put it. And it's more important, he said, to recognize the ugly fact that books are made from other books. And if you look at other books, like a play by Shakespeare, a lot of the time, there are women in them who make the men miserable. It's a common story element, he said in conclusion. Why single me out?

To be fair, I interjected. To be fair, Mack, you are the writer who's here talking to us. It only makes sense that you would be the one to be asked this question, given your prominence and the fact that we're Skyping.

I see, said Craig. All right.

Craig took a drink of water. He looked down, for a second, like he was thinking of what to say next.

You know, Professor, he said. It looks different when you lay it out for me like that. Now I get it.

Okay, I said. I think we have time for one more question.

No, Professor. Let me ask you something.

Okay.

Answer this question for me. Why aren't you more prominent in your field? Why are you teaching a bunch of bums in a backwater school like the one you're at? What did you do to deserve that?

Mack, I said. I don't agree with what you've said at all. I think this institution deserves better than that, and so do the students.

I'll tell you what you deserve, he said. You deserve a bullet in your fucking brain.

As soon as Craig had said that he looked stunned. He looked down. I'm sorry, he said. I didn't mean that.

I was stunned, too, and so were the students. We just looked up at the screen, at the impersonator who had said a terrible thing for no apparent reason. It was no wonder Craig had never done any commercials.

I think it's time we thank you, Mack, I finally said, for talking with us. It's been enlightening.

All right, he said, nodding fast, probably wondering if I would still pay him for his appearance.

Of course I would pay him. What if I didn't, and he told someone the truth about this situation? I'd be ruined.

I severed our connection, turned on the lights, and told everyone it was time to go.

There wasn't much of an aftermath, though I felt certain there would be one. I thought the next time we met the students would complain about it as readily as they'd complained about everything else. But they didn't mention it, and I didn't want to bring it up.

We carried on. We talked about *The Road*, and I acted like I hadn't lied to them elaborately twice that month.

I couldn't say that the conversation with Craig had worked in my favor, not in any definite way. But I did have a vague sense that, after the staged conversation with Cormac McCarthy, the students regarded me slightly differently than they had before. They didn't talk to each other in whispers when I was talking, as they had been doing all semester.

I thought I saw Riley the girl taking actual notes, on one day.

What was this about, I wondered. Were they convinced of my expertise, now? Had I fooled them, as I had fooled no one else in my career as a bad professor? Would it be a good idea to Skype with a fake author in every class I taught from now on?

We had productive conversations, in the couple of weeks that followed, about *The Road*. A memorable one concerned the people in the basement who need help and don't get it. It was surreal. Addison said she didn't expect the novel to present its characters with such a moral quandary.

It seems, she said, like in McCarthy's other novels he presents his characters with suffering, and then more of that, and violence and things.

Phillip nodded throughout this. There's a lot of feeling in it, too, he said. This guy's finally made me feel something. I have sympathy for the people in the basement. I feel even worse for the man and his son.

But there's no other way for it to go, said Pygmalion. If they suddenly liberated those cow people from the basement and were heroes, I would throw this book across the room.

I couldn't believe it. I didn't know what Pygmalion meant by calling them *cow people*, but the students were not only saying things, they were saying them to one another. It didn't matter that I disagreed with everything they said or questioned the relevance of Phillip's feelings to anything. It didn't matter that he'd spoken in violation of the affective fallacy. Their minds, it was clear, were active.

For a little while I remembered what had made me want to teach literature in the first place, those fleeting moments when, after so many long minutes spent trying to get a class session off the ground, the whole thing lifts suddenly, improbably, and there's real communication taking place between the people in the room. It's not just me bellowing insights into the abyss. Suddenly, the room lights up anew. Everyone cares, and you can feel it. You could feel it, that day, in that room, when we discussed *The Road* and more students than not had clearly read the material and had brought their minds into the room with them.

I left that room feeling a way I hadn't felt in a long time. I wished the class hadn't had to end. I wished we'd had more time to discuss what we'd discussed. It felt good, to feel this way again, after years of not feeling much at all. It also felt very bad, to not have felt that feeling for as long as it had been.

A week later, our last day arrived. There was supposed to be a final exam, a week after that, but this was our final day together as a regular class.

I like to make the last day casual. No more dead babies and guts and cannibalism in books. Instead we would have doughnuts and coffee, provided by me, the benevolent professor.

It's what I do at the end of all my classes. I bring enough for everyone and share what I bring with them all. If I didn't share, it would be rude and weird, and there was no way I could eat all those doughnuts without getting sick.

Riley the girl thanked me, and the others nodded in agreement with her thanking me, their mouths full of doughnuts.

Their mouths still full, I handed out their evaluation forms, gave them the necessary instructions, and left the room.

I can't be in the room when they fill them out, or else they might take my presence to be coercive. This was a rule even before I had a gun.

I sat outside the door, on a bench that was right there, outside the door. I gazed at my brown shoes for a minute. I was thinking about a lot of different things.

One thing I thought about was that I shouldn't have eaten a glazed doughnut. I should have gone with plain, because plain doughnuts aren't as bad for the human body as the glazed ones are.

I thought about how I didn't really like teaching anymore. It wasn't just that my career had required me to start carrying a gun, which had altered my relationship with the world and driven away someone (Shirley) who had loved me. There was more: I'd spent a whole semester teaching work I wasn't really passionate about, and there was no passion left. I found no joy in teaching. It was gone. The students had leached it right out of me.

It wasn't their fault. Their lives in education had been joyless all along; they'd never been presented with something that might stimulate them; they'd been given test after test for years, and then been presented, by me, with weird novels to read. Of course that didn't go well.

I thought about how it wasn't too late for me, how I could turn in my gun and my Ph.D. and do something else with the rest of my life. I could be a paralegal. I could change the world. I could change myself.

I was thinking of moving away, back to my hometown. My parents weren't dead yet. I could live near them, and figure something out.

I was wondering why the students were taking so long to evaluate me in there, when I heard an unusually loud bang come from the floor below. I heard the sound of boots on a staircase, pounding hard. I felt the footsteps vibrate under my feet.

My hand leapt to my gun in its shoulder holster.

I didn't think about it. I didn't think at all. My body recognized what was happening before my mind did.

I knew it was the gunman before I even saw him. I knew the sound of his footsteps from how they'd echoed across my nightmares for years.

I sat on the bench in the hallway and didn't breathe. I took the gun from its holster and watched the double doors at the end of the hallway. We'd kept them shut ever since the passage of Teach and Carry, I'm not sure why. I watched the doors and hunched there, leaning forward on the bench with my gun in my hand. I feared the worst.

The worst swung the doors open with another bang as he kicked them. I watched and didn't know what I was watching at the same time that I recognized Death when I saw him in his armor.

It was wrong to call him the gunman, I knew now. He wasn't a man. He was a mockup of a man, an accumulation of limbs and equipment in the shape of a man. He was steel and Kevlar, a motorcycle helmet atop limbs wrapped blackly, dressed to kill.

I saw an assault rifle.

I was sitting at the far end of the hall, the other set of double doors behind me. I had my pistol in my hand, and to tell the rest I must rely on the accounts of others, of forensics reports and witnesses who saw nothing but heard all that there was to hear from the level underneath ours.

I fired my gun at the gunman, they say. I have forgotten the act of doing it. I fired five times before I burst through the doors behind me and barely saved myself.

Two of my bullets hit the gunman, one in his upper right arm, where the Kevlar body armor he'd bought on eBay stopped it. The other bullet grazed his face, though graze isn't quite the word for it as it doesn't do justice to what it did.

I watched a videographic of the bullet's trajectory, later, on CNN, in the hospital. In slow motion, I watched the bullet burst through the facemask of his motorcycle helmet, which is not meant for stopping bullets, and from there veer into the gunman's videographic face as it blasted open his cheekbone and made its way just past his brain and back out the side of his head, lodging itself in his helmet.

It didn't stop him. I don't know how it didn't.

I will not write his name and perpetuate his infamy. He murdered all nine of the students in my classroom. There was supposed to be a larger class being held down the hall, which would have meant at least a dozen more fatalities, but the class was cancelled that morning, and the other classrooms were empty because enrollments had been so low that the courses that would have been meeting in those rooms had long since been called off. All of my students were in class that day because I'd promised them doughnuts and coffee. They had made certain not to miss that.

I don't know who died first. I wasn't there anymore. After I unloaded my gun, they said on CNN, I ran to the stairwell behind me and promptly fell headfirst down the staircase, knocking myself out. It's why I don't remember the gunman's rifle going off and the students' cries for mercy. I don't know who took the first bullet, or how much time elapsed before Riley the girl leapt from the window to her death on the pavement below.

If I'd made it out of the building conscious, and called the police, it would have made no difference. It took him twenty-five seconds to kill them all. The gunman put a bullet through his own head as soon as he'd finished with my students.

They said on the news that it was thanks to me that he killed himself after killing only nine people. They said that although I didn't save my students, surely I had saved others. The bullet I'd put in his face, they said, slowed him down. He must have known, they said, that he hadn't much farther to go.

The gunman had been a student at the school, no one I had known. According to a diary he kept in his dorm room, his plan had been to start with the top floor and work his way down, through the rest of the building, killing everyone.

It was a bad plan. Everyone ran from the building as soon as they heard the shots upstairs, so that even if he'd made his way to the floor below ours, he would have found only empty classrooms. I guess that's the caliber of student we have to work with now, I told Daniel when he came to see me at the hospital.

He didn't laugh. Neither did I. He told me I had bruises on my face. They're just all over, he said, wincing. I told him I knew that already.

I knew what Daniel wanted to say but didn't. I knew he wanted to remind me what he'd said when I'd chosen my gun, that five bullets weren't enough, that it wasn't unlikely that I'd miss five times. What will you do with an obsolete gun like that, he had said, when the man you're up against has an assault rifle?

I slept a lot, in the hospital. I dreamed I was still in the hallway where I'd failed to stop the gunman. I felt, when I was awake, like I was still there. Like I would not be allowed to leave, ever.

When Daniel came to see me, we discussed my evaluations. He usually dropped them in my mailbox without comment, but these, he said, were worth talking about.

Here? I said.

He nodded. He handed them to me.

Only half of them were there, he said. He said the other half were soaked with blood and kept as evidence.

Daniel watched as I read the four evaluations that had survived the massacre, my aching head in one of my hands. Each evaluation was at least a full page, and each was an account of what an atrocious semester it had been for the students, how they had suffered through the dull lectures that Riley the girl (I recognized the handwriting) called *pointless* and Riley the boy said were *mind-numbing*.

They objected to the reading selections, claiming that the course description has misled them to think they would read interesting books from around the world and not *a bunch of shit about horses*, wrote Addison, who didn't hold back, and whose evaluation was the best piece of writing she'd done all semester.

Addison, I'd learned, was the only student who'd tried to stop the gunman. She had attended the optional on-campus training for active shooter situations. As soon as the murderer stepped through the door, she threw her copy of *The Road* at him. She threw her desk at him. It is what they told her to do. They told her that even a futile act of resistance was better than no resistance at all, in cases like this one. Not that it did her any good. It has a chance of working only when more than one person does it. She was the only one to do it.

Phillip's evaluation of me was the most insightful, and the most precise in its excoriation. It revealed what I had suspected all along: that Phillip was the sharpest tack in a classroom full of tacks that were all sharp enough in their own ways but that had been dulled beyond hope by years of public education.

He had known that the *Nightstalker* pages were a fabrication. He confessed to having uploaded them to Tumblr.

He probably thought I wouldn't know it was he who had confessed, because evaluations were anonymous. He didn't know I would know him by his handwriting. He said he didn't understand the purpose in forcing (his word) students to Skype with a Cormac McCarthy impersonator.

That threw me. He had known it wasn't really Cormac McCarthy they spoke to. Which made me wonder if the other students knew it was not McCarthy they spoke to, knew it was Craig they were talking with and yet played along.

Phillip had written pages of material. It was no wonder they had taken so long to evaluate me. They must have all sat there watching Phillip write until their murderer burst through the door.

I want to talk with the professor about this, Phillip had written. *I want to have a dialogue about this and maybe we can both learn from this semester. The professor seems like he's rough around the edges, but I know he is going somewhere.*

If Phillip hadn't been killed, I would have found this condescending. I would have thought Phillip was out of line. But it broke my heart.

I looked up at Daniel, who wasn't looking at me. I don't know, he said. I don't know.

I breathed deeply, loudly enough that Daniel could hear the breath I took.

I don't know, he said again, what possessed you to do this. If what they wrote is true. He looked at me, to see if I would shake my head or otherwise deny the evaluation's allegation. I didn't. He sighed. It doesn't make any sense, he said.

He didn't speak for a while, and I didn't speak, until he said, Listen. It's like I said before. This semester's not one to repeat. But it's one to learn from.

I quit, I said.

213

Daniel looked at me, incredulous.

I can't go back into a classroom, I said. You know that. I can't teach in a warzone. I don't know how I lasted as long as I did.

I had had a lot of time to think, at the hospital, alone in my room at night and in the day. As soon as I woke up there, some hours after knocking myself out on the stairs, I knew I wasn't a teacher anymore. How could I be?

It was the gun massacre I'd failed to prevent that convinced me I was unfit for the modern classroom. How could another roomful of students trust me?

I also had a dream about Shirley. We were in my apartment again, and we were talking, I don't know what about. I don't think there were any words in the dream, but there was a feeling, and a good one, one I hadn't felt since she'd gone. Teaching, and the things it brought with it now, had driven her away.

I didn't tell Daniel about the dream. He would have laughed at that, just as he laughed at my saying I couldn't teach in a warzone.

You think a classroom hasn't always been a warzone? he said. You think this is new?

I sighed and rubbed my eyes. I pressed my head against my pillow. I know what you're trying to do, I said. You want to say what's implied by the epigraphs to *Blood Meridian*.

Daniel looked puzzled, but I knew what I was talking about. I was also repeating something that Phillip had written in his evaluation. He had spent a short paragraph refuting what's implied by the epigraphs to *Blood Meridian*.

You think, I said, speaking from the heart, but also paraphrasing Phillip, that people have always been barbarians. That we always will be savages. When there's a shooting, you say, *Right. That's how it is. It's what we pretend to not be but always are*. But, Christ, Daniel. That's not how it is. I sat up and looked him in the eyes. That's not how I'm able to see it, I said. To see things that way, I'd have to give up completely. Give up on hope. On life. If I'm going to continue living, I have to believe there's more to us than monsters.

Daniel was frowning. He was glaring, but then his glare took a turn for the resigned. He was quiet for a long time. Try telling that, he finally said, with a sigh, to your World Literature class.

We kept talking. Daniel reminded me of certain things: how hard I'd worked to get my job; how many years I'd spent in school so I'd be qualified to get it; how hard it was to get tenure, which I had done; how unlikely it was that I'd find a good job with a Ph.D. in English; what a privileged place I was in. There aren't many of us left, he said.

I listened. Daniel could be convincing. He talked me into an unpaid leave arrangement, in the hope that after a year of research and trauma recovery I would be rejuvenated and return to teach again. I don't know what I will do.

A few days after I left the hospital, the President of the college gave me an award. For my service, he said. At the ceremony, someone from the NRA gave me a certificate. I have not read the certificate.

At the same event, the parents of two of the students, Riley the boy and Phillip, approached me and thanked me personally for attempting to save their children. They had tears streaming from their eyes.

I thought Phillip's mother would die in front of me when I said her son was the brightest student I had met in my career. I don't think I was lying. She wept, and I wept. Her husband had to carry her away.

I stood there alone, once they were gone. No one came to carry me away.

Thank You

Thank you to Saba Razvi, for choosing this book for Sundress. Thank you to the readers who saw something in the collection and moved it forward through the reading process. Thank you to Erin Elizabeth Smith, for inventing Sundress Publications and making it the great press it is. Thank you to all the people at Sundress whose names I don't know, who keep it going. You work hard.

Thank you to Kate McIntyre, who read an early version of this book, and helped decide what to cut, what order to put the stories in, and what to call the thing when it was done. You helped make this book what it is.

Thank you to Joe Aguilar, Joanna Luloff, Stephanie Carpenter, and Meagan Ciesla. You are brilliant, and I have learned an awful lot from you.

Thank you to Christine Gosnay, for your insights on "Gunmen" and for being a good friend.

Thank you Maureen Stanton, Christine Sneed, and Sara Pritchard, for offering kind words in support of this collection.

A fellowship from the Virginia Center for the Creative Arts helped to make this book possible. Thank you, Virginia Center for the Creative Arts.

Thank you, Stefanie, for working so hard and being so damn good. I'd have lost my mind without you. I might still.

Thank you to Rose and Moriah. You make life harder, but you make life better.

Thank you Mom and Dad, Jimmy, David, Sam, Will, Anne, Owen, Miles, Winnie, Becky, Charlie, Karen, Corey, Rob, Robb, Marc, Camellia, Tim, Will, Alex, and everyone I owe thanks to who isn't mentioned here.

About the Author

Robert Long Foreman's first book, *Among Other Things*, a collection of essays, won the inaugural Robert C. Jones Prize for Short Prose and was published by Pleiades Press in 2017. His first novel, *Weird Pig*, won the Nilsen Prize for a First Novel. He has won a Pushcart prize and has published work in magazines that include *AGNI, Crazyhorse, Kenyon Review Online, Copper Nickel,* and *The Cincinnati Review.* He earned a PhD in English-Creative Writing at the University of Missouri in 2012. Born and raised in Wheeling, West Virginia, he lives in Kansas City. Find more at robertlongforeman.com.

Other Sundress Prose Titles

The Butterfly Lady
Danny M. Hoey Jr.
$16